KU-356-322

# The Nutmeg Tree

LINKS HOTEL, BRORA.

# The Nutmeg Tree

## by *Margery Sharp*

**This complete and unabridged new edition is produced in full compliance with wartime regulations.**

NEW YORK
GROSSET & DUNLAP — *Publishers*
*By arrangement with Little, Brown, and Company*

COPYRIGHT 1937, BY MARGERY SHARP

ALL RIGHTS RESERVED, INCLUDING THE RIGHT
TO REPRODUCE THIS BOOK OR PORTIONS
THEREOF IN ANY FORM

PRINTED IN THE UNITED STATES OF AMERICA

# The Nutmeg Tree

# Chapter 1

Julia, by marriage Mrs. Packett, by courtesy Mrs. Macdermot, lay in her bath singing the Marseillaise. Her fine robust contralto, however, was less resonant than usual; for on this particular summer morning the bathroom, in addition to the ordinary fittings, contained a lacquer coffee table, seven hatboxes, half a dinner service, a small grandfather clock, all Julia's clothes, a single-bed mattress, thirty-five novelettes, three suitcases, and a copy of a Landseer stag. The customary echo was therefore lacking; and if the ceiling now and then trembled, it was not because of Julia's song, but because the men from the Bayswater Hire Furniture Company had not yet finished removing the hired furniture.

On the other side of the door an occasional shuffling of feet showed that the two broker's men had not even one chair to sit on.

Thus beleaguered, Julia sang. With every breath she drew in a generous diaphragmful of verbena-scented steam, and let it out again in the form of equally generous chest-notes. She did this not out of defiance, nor to keep her spirits up, but because at that time of the morning song was natural to her. The belligerence of her tones was due simply to the belligerence of the melody: her choice of the melody was due simply to the fact that she had received, the night before, a letter from France.

So Julia sang, until in the pause before the reprise a weary voice sounded huskily through the door.

"Ain't you done *yet*, mum?" demanded the voice.

"No," said Julia.

"But you bin in an hour 'n' 'arf already!" protested the voice.

Julia turned on the hot tap. She could stay in a bath almost indefinitely, and had often, during her periodic attempts at slimming, lain parboiled for two or three hours. But nothing — as was now plainly to be seen — had ever slimmed Julia. At thirty-nine, — only five feet, three inches in height, — she had a thirty-eight-inch bust, a thirty-one waist, and forty-one hips; and though these three vital points were linked by extremely agreeable curves, Julia nevertheless hankered after a fashionable toothpick silhouette. She hankered, but not consistently. Her comfortable flesh refused to be martyred. It regarded orange juice as an appetizer, not as a staff of life; and as a result there lay Julia, — recumbent in her cloud of steam, rosy-

— 4 —

pink with heat, — looking like the presiding goddess
of some baroque ceiling.

The door rattled.

"If you break in," called Julia, turning off the tap,
"I'll have you up for assault!"

A dead silence showed that the threat had taken effect. There was a muffled consultation; then a second
voice, even wearier than the first, resumed the argument.

"It's only five pound, mum," pleaded the voice. "We
don't want to give no trouble — "

"Then go away," retorted Julia.

"We can't, mum. It's our duty. If you'll just let us
take the stuff — or better still, pay us the five pound — "

"I haven't got five pounds," said Julia truthfully;
and for the first time her brow clouded. She hadn't got
one pound: she possessed exactly seven-and-eightpence,
and she had to leave for France in the morning. For
perhaps five minutes she lay and pondered, considering,
one after the other, all those persons from whom she had
borrowed money in the past. She thought also of those
to whom she had lent; but one set was as hopeless as
the other. With real regret, she thought of the late Mr.
Macdermot. And at last she thought of Mr. Lewis.

"Hey!" called Julia. "You know that antique-shop
at the end of the road?"

The bailiffs consulted.

"We know a pawnbroker's, mum. Name of Lewis."

"That's it," admitted Julia, "but it's an antique-shop as well. One of you nip along and fetch Mr. Lewis here. He'll pay you."

They consulted again; but after waiting (upright) for two hours, they were ready to clutch at a straw. Julia heard the tread of departing feet, and the shuffle of the feet that remained. Then she dried her hands, lit a cigarette, and reached out to the coffee table for a letter with a French stamp.

## 2

Though it had arrived only the previous night, she already knew it by heart.

My dear Mother, —

It seems strange that you won't know my writing. I am sending this through the Bank, and unless you are abroad you ought to get it almost at once. Could you come out here and see me? It is a long way, but a beautiful place, high up on the edge of Haute Savoie, and we shall be here till October. But I would like you to come (if you can) at once. Grandmother also invites you, to stay as long as you like. As you may know, she and Sir William Waring are now my trustees. The point is [here the small, neat writing grew suddenly larger] that I want to get married, and Grandmother objects. I know there are all sorts of legal complications, but after all you are my mother, and you ought to be consulted. If you can come, the best way is by the 11:40 P.M. from Paris to Ambérieu, where a car will meet you. I do hope it will be possible.

Your affectionate daughter,—

SUSAN PACKETT.

From a girl of twenty, in love, to her mother, the letter was hardly expansive; but Julia understood. Because of a variety of circumstances, she had not seen her daughter for sixteen years; and the bare fact that that daughter now remembered and appealed to her was so exquisitely touching that even now, on rereading the letter for the twentieth time, Julia dropped a tear or two into the bath. But they were tears of sentiment, not of sorrow; at the thought of a trip to France, of a love affair to be handled, her spirits soared. "CATCHING TRAIN THURSDAY ALL LOVE MOTHER," she had wired back; and only then had she remembered her unusually disastrous economic situation. She had no money, no proper wardrobe, and a creditor about to foreclose. But none of these things mattered, when Susan wanted her. Susan wanted her, Susan was unhappy, and to Susan she would go. . . .

"But she was christened Suzanne!" thought Julia suddenly; and was still staring at the signature when she was brought back to the present by the welcome sound of Mr. Lewis' voice.

"My dear Julia!" he shouted. "What is all this that you fetch me for? You are not really drowning yourself? This man — "

"He's a bailiff," called Julia. "They're both bailiffs. Send them away."

After a few moments the heavy footsteps retreated, the lighter ones returned.

"Now, Julia, what is it? These men — "

"Have they gone?"

"Gone and glad to," replied Mr. Lewis. "They are very modest men, my dear, and so am I. But they haven't gone farther than the stairs."

"Can they hear us?"

"They can hear me if I shout for help. They seem to think that there is stuff in there besides the usual fittings."

"There is," said Julia. "That's what I want you for. There's stuff in here I've got to sell — *good* stuff — and you've always been a sport to me, Joe, so I'm giving you first chance. There's a real lacquer table, and a new mattress, and a genuine antique grandfather clock, and a lovely dinner service, and a picture of a stag that's a real painting. I'll take thirty quid for the lot."

"Not from me you won't," said Mr. Lewis.

Julia sat up with a splash.

"Of all the old Jews! Why, the stag's worth that alone, and I didn't mean to include it. I'm offering you the table and the clock and a new mattress and a dinner service, and dirt cheap at that."

"Well, let me look at 'em," said Mr. Lewis patiently.

"Of course you can't look at them. I'm in the bath."

"You mean you want me to buy blind?"

"That's it," agreed Julia. "Have a flutter."

Mr. Lewis reflected. He was a man who liked to get everything cut and dried.

"You mean you will sell me, for thirty pounds, stuff I haven't even seen, which is probably worth twenty-five bob, and which already belongs to whatever fool has been giving you credit?"

"That's right," said Julia cheerfully, "except that it's worth more like sixty, and I only owe five. What's your favourite tune?"

"The Blue Danube," said Mr. Lewis.

Julia sang it.

3

Half an hour passed. The men from the Bayswater Hire Furniture Company had taken themselves and the hired furniture away. A man from the Gas Company had come and cut off the gas. But the bailiffs remained, and so did Mr. Lewis; for even through a bolted door Julia's personality triumphed. When she was tired of singing she entertained them with anecdotes of her early life on the stage; when she ran out of anecdotes she imitated film stars, and so successfully that the grandfather clock, chiming for noon, took them all by surprise.

"That the genuine antique?" asked Mr. Lewis with interest.

"Yes," said Julia, returning promptly to business. "Now listen, Joe: I've got to go to France first thing in the morning. I've got to have ten pounds for my return fare, and a fiver for these toughs. That's fifteen quid, and I haven't a rag to my back. Make it eighteen-ten, and I'll throw in the stag."

"Fourteen," said Mr. Lewis.

"Seventeen," said Julia. "Be a sport!"

"Be a sport, guv'nor!" echoed the bailiffs — now definitely on Julia's side.

Mr. Lewis felt himself weaken. A coffee table, a dinner service, a mattress, and a grandfather clock — it all depended on the clock. The chimes had been good ones, and if it looked like an antique to Julia it would probably look like an antique to most people. It might even *be* an antique, and old grandfathers fetched a lot of money. . . .

Julia had known what she was about when she appealed to his gambling instincts.

"Sixteen-ten," said Mr. Lewis. "Take it or leave it."

"Done!" said Julia; and at last got out of the bath.

# Chapter 2

The first time Julia had seen her future husband by daylight was on a spring morning in 1916, when she woke at about half-past ten to find him still sleeping at her side. She knew his name, Sylvester Packett, and that he was a first lieutenant in the Gunners; and in spite of the fact that for six consecutive nights he had danced with her from twelve till four in the morning, that was all she did know. He was the most silent boy she had ever met; not even champagne loosened his tongue; and she had regretfully (but philosophically) come to the conclusion that he danced with her simply because he couldn't sleep. Boys got like that, in 1916; she wouldn't be a bit surprised if he'd come back with her the night before just to see if he could get some sleep *that* way. . . . Julia, at eighteen, considered this idea without either surprise or rancour: it was simply, like so many other things, the War.

"Poor boy!" said Julia under her breath; for she was easily sentimental, and cried over a casualty list whenever she saw one. The young man stirred in his sleep, sighed, and slept again. He had four more days' leave, and if only he stayed with her — thought Julia — he should sleep like that every single night. . . .

Sylvester Packett stayed. He wanted to be down in Suffolk, but in Suffolk he couldn't sleep, and with Julia he could. It was unfortunate, but it was the War. He stayed for four more days, and at the end of that time was swallowed back into France.

Julia wept when he went. Her affection had been at least disinterested, for she refused all gifts except a Gunner brooch. But it was also ephemeral; save for one awkward and unexpected circumstance, she would never have thought of him again.

2

At the beginning of August, after a five-hour chorus rehearsal for "Pretty Louise," Julia fainted. When her friends had brought her round, and after she had taken expert advice, she went home and wrote to Sylvester.

There was nothing of the blackmailer about her. The letter said simply that she was going to have a baby, and she was sure it was his, and if he could lend her a hand she would be very much obliged, but if not he wasn't to worry. "With love and best wishes,

Julia." In answer she received the shock of her life. He came home and married her.

He did it during a forty-eight-hour leave, and never in her life did Julia pass a more uncomfortable two days. What with relief and gratification her spirits, never low, had soared to an unexampled pitch; but he managed to damp them. He was no longer silent, but he was deadly. He talked to her for hours on end about a dreary-sounding place in Suffolk — an old, old house called Barton, in an old garden, in a village ten miles from a railway station, where his people had apparently lived, without either a car or a telephone, for hundreds and hundreds of years. He would actually have taken her there, but for lack of time; yet when Julia, happy in her escape and anxious to console, projected a visit for his next leave, he at once bit on the knuckle of his thumb and changed the subject. He behaved, in fact, as though the future had ceased to affect him. He wouldn't even buy shirts. To cheer him up Julia insisted on dining at the Ritz and going to a musical comedy; but even these measures were useless.

And if the evening was a failure, the wedding night was a flop.

Julia spent it alone. All night long her husband sat up writing a letter. It was addressed to his people, but not directly; the Bank had instructions, he said, to forward it at the proper time. When this letter was read, it was found to consist of detailed instructions for the bringing-up of his unborn child, to which he referred throughout as "the boy." The boy was to be born at Barton, and to receive the name of Henry Sylvester. He was to remain at Barton till the age of nine, then to go to a preparatory school for Winchester. After Winchester, on making his choice between the Army and Medicine, he was to proceed to either Sandhurst or Cambridge. If undecided, he was to choose the Army. "But on no account," wrote his father, with unsuspected dryness, "is he to become an Army Doctor."

Such was the main outline; there were also provisions for a pony — "which must be exchanged as soon as the boy outgrows it; there is nothing worse for a child than to feel his feet trailing on the ground" — and for coaching in cricket during the summer holidays. At twelve the boy was to be given his father's old 20-bore; at eighteen, the Purdey 12: his grandfather would teach him how to handle them. All these things, and many others, had been thought of, pondered over, and put down on paper; with corrections, interlinings and much copying-out; for in this long, detailed and comprehensive document, far more than in his official will, was embodied the last testament of Sylvester Packett.

There was a brief codicil: —

I never told anybody, but there is usually a tit's nest in the old pump at the bottom of the orchard. Also a bulfinch's in the red May tree at the corner of the big field. Tell him the great thing in blowing is to go *slow*. You will of course never take more than one egg.

Your loving father, —

SYLVESTER PACKETT.

Two months later he was killed at Ypres; and the child born at Barton was a girl.

3

She was christened Suzanne Sylvester. The first name was chosen by Julia as both patriotic (being French) and pretty; and the Packetts let her have her way. They were unbelievably good to her. As the mother of their grandchild (even of the wrong sex) they accepted her with open arms. Affectionately, unquestioningly, she was installed as the daughter of the house. All they asked was that she and the child should stay there and be happy.

And Julia tried. For nineteen months the lay figure of young Mrs. Packett did the flowers, paid calls, went to church, and played with the baby whenever the nurse allowed. Night after night this lay figure sat at dinner with its father- and mother-in-law; every night, for an hour afterwards, it played easy classics on the drawing-room piano. At such mild festivities as the neighbourhood afforded it played the same pieces on the pianos of its hosts. All its evening dresses had backs to them, and two had long sleeves.

Such was the puppet constructed by Julia's gratitude; and gratitude alone pulled its strings. Julia herself sat in young Mrs. Packett's room and wept for boredom; but even her tears, when discovered, were taken as one more sign of the puppet's faithful and tender heart. But Julia's heart was tender too: one of the worst elements in her boredom was the lack of someone to love. She had her child, indeed, and was very fond of it; but "someone," to Julia, meant a man. Loving some man or other was her natural function: only the man had to be alive, and there, and kissing her back. Love for a memory — even for the memory of a husband — was right out of Julia's line. . . .

It must be admitted that to have held out as she did, under such conditions, for a year and seven months, was extremely creditable; and no less so because at the end of that time she gave up the struggle and went thoroughly back to the bad.


4

The bad, originally, was crowd-work in a comedy film, which Julia heard of through a girl-friend who had a boy-friend who knew a man in the then struggling British film industry. She met the girl-friend at Selfridge's, on one of her rare expeditions to Town; they encountered each other (in the stocking department) shortly after three; but what with having tea, and talking over old times, and having dinner, and going to the Bodega to meet the boy-friend, and then going on to meet *his* friend at the Café Royal, Julia missed the last train back. She spent the night at the girl-friend's flat, sleeping delightedly on the sofa in a bathrobe that smelt of grease paint; and that night, and that smell, settled her future. The next morning, at Barton, she told her parents-in-law that she was going back to live in Town.

"But — Susan?" said Mrs. Packett quickly.

Julia hesitated. Her husband's letter, now locked in Mrs. Packett's jewel-case, had been written on the assumption that the child was to be a son; but it was still a sort of gospel. Ponies, particularly Shetlands, were old Henry Packett's constant preoccupation, as the educational requirements of Girton were the preoccupation of his wife. . . .

"The child must of course stay here," said Henry Packett, speaking his thought.

"If Julia can bear to be separated — " began his wife more tactfully.

Julia felt that she could. Those nineteen months of

being young Mrs. Packett had exhausted her supply of maternal affection; and she was also aware that for a young child the life at Barton was far more suitable than the life she herself looked forward to, in Town. She hadn't yet any definite plans about it, but she hoped and trusted that it would be very unsuitable indeed.

"Well — if she won't be too much trouble — "

"Trouble!" cried Mrs. Packett joyfully. "Isn't this her home? — As it's yours too, my dear, whenever you choose to come to it."

After that, all went smoothly. They disapproved, they were sorry, but they were unalterably good. Their patriotism had not permitted Julia to draw her pension; she had lived at Barton as a daughter, with a daughter's dress-allowance; and this was now made up to three hundred a year. Julia, obscurely conscience-stricken, thought it too much, but the Packetts were adamant. They had apparently no opinion of her earning powers, and their son's widow could not possibly live on less. That was her portion, she must take it; and whenever she wished, she was to come back to her home.

## 5

During the next year she went back five times. The year after, she went down for her daughter's birthday, but did not stay the night. On subsequent birthdays she wrote. But when Susan was nine Julia had a sudden burst of maternity and invited the child for a week's sight-seeing in Town. The opportunity was a good one, for Mr. Macdermot, whose flat Julia then shared, had been called to Menton by an invalid wife; but Susan did not come, and in answer to her invitation Julia received a counterproposal of some importance.

The Packetts were prepared, they wrote, to take complete responsibility for the child's present, and to make her their heiress in the future, if Julia on her side would renounce all legal claim. Should she do so, she would of course see Susan whenever she wished, either at Barton or wherever else the grandparents decided; but she could not, without permission, take the child away alone. This last pill was gilded by a warm invitation from Mrs. Packett to come down at once and stay for a month.

Julia considered both these proposals carefully, accepted the first and rejected the second. She was only too glad to have her daughter's future so fully and agreeably secured, but she didn't want any renunciation scene. Also she was very busy, having interested herself, in a rather lofty, lady-patroness manner, in a new touring company then being organized by one of her theatrical friends. She would come down soon, she told the Packetts, but not just then.

Two months later she heard from them again. After that decent interval they presented her with a lump sum of seven thousand pounds in Government Stock, to take the place of her allowance. This surprising generosity Julia unresentfully interpreted as a desire to be finally rid of her; but she was only half right. It was, also, a salve to Mrs. Packett's conscience. "With some money of her own," said Mrs. Packett (who had the frank, old-fashioned viewpoint), "she'll be able to get herself a husband."

Julia did not get a husband, but she went into management. She put on two plays within six months; and when the second came off there remained, of the seven thousand pounds, exactly nineteen-and-six.

6

The death of Mr. Macdermot some three years later thus left Julia in a very precarious position. She was thirty-one, too old (and also too plump) to go back to the chorus; she had acquired comfortable if not luxurious tastes, and she was completely untrained for any of the respectably remunerative professions. But she managed. She was very versatile. She still got a certain amount of crowd-work, and was once (in a night-club scene) the Lady Who Fell into the Fountain. Now and again at mannequin parades she showed Models for the Fuller Figure. Her cheerful smile advertised a new baking powder and a Tonic for Women over Forty. Also, of course, she borrowed from gentleman friends, of whom she had a great many, and occasionally she accepted their hospitality. The only thing Julia never once considered was a return to Barton and the Packetts.

She was cut off from them forever. With real humility she weighed herself up, and looked at herself all round, and acknowledged that she wasn't good enough for them. Certainly she wasn't good enough for a daughter who (as Mrs. Packett once reported) went to school at Wycombe Abbey, and who had riding lessons, and whose great friend was the daughter of a lord. . . .

So Julia settled the matter in her mind, and for months on end (being extremely occupied and always hard-up) quite forgot she had a daughter at all.

It was only when Susan was in trouble that Julia's maternal instincts suddenly reawoke; but they did so to some purpose. Their immediate effect, as has been seen, was the embarrassment of two bailiffs, and the swindling of Mr. Lewis.

# Chapter 3

The address from which Susan had written was *Les Sapins, Muzin, près de Belley, Ain;* and as soon as the flat was once more at her disposal Julia went through her clothes to see which, if any, were suited to such a destination. It was in the country, of course, like Barton, and probably much the same sort of place; only naturally gayer, through being in France. Julia spread out her three evening dresses and looked at them thoughtfully: there was a midnight-blue taffeta — its bodice all boned-up to dispense with shoulder straps — which a scarf or coatee would possibly make do; but over the other two — one white, the top consisting chiefly of a black velvet poppy; one green, with sequins — Julia shook her head; even in France, the Packetts wouldn't be as gay as *that*.

"I've got to look like a lady," she thought. "I've got to *be* a lady. . . ."

The idea at once alarmed and braced her. It would be difficult, but she could do it. And on one point, indeed, Julia was more fortunate than she knew: her conception of the ladylike was as clear-cut, as lacking in ambiguous shades and small subtleties, as a dressmaker's diagram; and like a dressmaker's diagram, it was concerned with surface effects only. Nature's ladies were no ladies to Julia. They were good sorts, which was a very different thing. If you had suddenly asked Julia for a definition, she would probably have replied, Ladies never drink with their mouths full, and never pick anyone up. If you had asked her why not, she would have replied, Because they are ladies. If then, with discourteous persistence, you enquired whether one must wait to see a woman eating and drinking, or being given the glad-eye, before one could tell, Julia would have enlarged her definition. You could always tell a lady by her clothes. However smart, the clothes of a true lady never hit you in the eye; and if she suddenly wanted to change her underwear — you would of course have had to get this bit out of Julia before she became a lady herself — she always could.

In the end Julia decided to take single instead of return tickets, and to buy a new dinner dress with the money saved. She also purchased a linen suit, a Matron's Model hat, and three pairs of camiknickers. She had indeed plenty of these already, but all with policemen embroidered on the legs. And on the platform at Victoria, for almost the first time in her life, she bought a book.

It was *The Forsyte Saga,* and Julia chose it partly because it seemed such a lot for the money, and partly because she had often heard Galsworthy spoken of as a Good Author. She fancied it was the sort of book Susan would like to see her mother reading; and Julia's maternal affection was so strong (though admittedly erratic) that she read three whole chapters between London and Dover.

## 2

Ladies, when travelling alone, never speak to anybody; so it was with but a stately inclination of the head that Julia thanked a naval officer who steadied her on the gangway and a commercial traveller who set up her deck-chair. She had no difficulty in selecting an isolated position, for passengers were few; and with her coat over her knees, and the *Saga* open on her lap, she settled comfortably down to get on with Literature.

A schoolmistress in a mackintosh, reconnoitring for a sheltered spot, approached and paused.

"It's out of the wind here?" she speculated.

Julia inclined her head.

"Because I think," said the schoolmistress — though more formally — "that we're in for a blow."

Julia inclined her head again. The schoolmistress passed on. Julia then (with a brief interval while she watched a Daimler being swung on board) read three chapters of *A Man of Property* straight off the reel. If she found the going a trifle stiff, that rather pleased her than otherwise, for it confirmed her opinion that she was reading a really good book; and then, no one could possibly be more of a lady than its heroine. To have all that S.A. and never get any fun out of it! What could be more ladylike than that? So read, so mused Julia, a lady herself for all the world to see; and hardly lifted her eyes from one paragraph to the next.

She could not help noticing, however, a certain group composed of one woman and five men who stood leaning over the rail almost directly opposite her chair. It was the proportion of the sexes that attracted her attention. One women to five men! Julia looked at her again, and saw nothing to merit such good fortune. She was short, plump, fifty if a day, with hair so violently golden, and lips so violently red, and such a drift of pale mauve powder on her nose, that not even an all-black ensemble could disguise her resemblance to a macaw. Julia really had to raise her eyebrows; but she also, before returning

to her book, spared a glance for the five men. They
varied in height from very tall to very short, but all
had the same broad shoulders, straight backs, and narrow hips; there was even a vague likeness in their
features, though the tallest (addressed as Fred) was
also by far the best-looking. He was one of the handsomest men Julia had ever seen.

"I believe they're theatricals," she thought; and at
that moment happened to catch Fred's eye. It was
light brown and boldly appreciative — just the sort
of eye that Julia liked. But she did not respond. "None
of that, now!" she adjured herself; and started dog-
gedly on Chapter Eight.

Literature still kept its precarious hold on her attention when the boat, which had hitherto proceeded
in a reasonable decorous manner, began to feel and
transmit the increasing motion of the sea. The chops
of the Channel were living up to their name, and
more than one passenger stumbled hastily by, to con-
tend with them below. Julia, in addition to many
other useful qualities, had that of being an excellent
sailor, and felt so little inconvenience that she decided to take a walk. Her feet were cold, and the
empty decks offered space for brisk motion. A little
unsteadily (in spite of her sea-legs) she walked twice
up and down, then discovered that the other side
would be more sheltered, and continued round. So

far was she from seeking companionship that the sight of a group of five men would at once have driven her back, but that their attitudes — of bewilderment and dismay — at once drew her on. They were grouped, so far as she could discern, round a deck-chair; and as she approached a series of loud female groans told her that the victim, whether of accident or *mal de mer,* was their lady companion. She lay perfectly still, huddled in a lumpy mass, so that for one wild moment Julia imagined that the Daimler must have got loose and run over her. But it was sea-sickness only, as a sudden convulsion just then showed; and as a steward hurried up the group loosened and Fred detached himself. Julia's ladylike inhibitions melted like snow.

"If you want any brandy," she said directly, "I've a flask in my bag."

But he shook his head.

"She's had too much already. It's the pork."

"She does seem bad," murmured Julia sympathetically. The relief of opening her mouth, of returning to the common level of humanity, was so great that it brought with it a genuine flow of interest and concern. Julia, at that moment, not only would have given the sufferer her brandy, she would have held the sufferer's head. There were two men holding it already, however, and only sympathy was required.

"She *is* bad," stated Fred. "That's Ma all over — all merry and bright till the last minute, then up it all comes and she thinks she's going to die. *They —*" he nodded over his shoulder at the four mourners — "*they* want to undo her stays; but she won't let 'em."

"And quite right," said Julia warmly. "The stomach wants holding together, not letting loose. You ought to do them up tighter."

"You can't do Ma's stays any tighter — not without killing her. I don't know how she breathes as it is." They listened a moment in respectful silence, as the lady's groans rose a sudden octave higher. "Wonderful lung-power, hasn't she?" asked Fred with gloomy pride. "She used to be able to sing 'The Lost Chord' upside-down."

"Theatricals?" asked Julia, pleased at her intuition.

With the neatness of a conjurer he produced his card. It was rather larger than usual, but then it had to be. "The Six Flying Genocchios," it announced: "Trapeze and High Wire. *Daring, Thrilling, Unbelievable. The Koh-i-Noor of Aerial Entertainment.*" The first line was printed in red, the second in silver, the third in blue; so that altogether it was a very imposing affair.

Julia had scarcely looked her admiration when a second card slipped over the first. On a smaller area, chastely engraved, she read the name and address of

Mr. Fred Genocchio, 5, Connaught Villas, Maida Vale.

"That's my personal one," said Fred. "You keep it."

Julia slipped it into her bag. She was slightly mortified at not having one of her own to give in exchange, and as Fred waited expectantly had to introduce herself by mere word of mouth.

"I'm Mrs. Macdermot. I'm going to join my daughter."

"In Paris?"

"No, in Haute Savoie." Julia was pleased about that: Haute Savoie sounded so much better — more travelled, more distinguished. She should really have said Ain, of course, but did not know how to pronounce it.

"That's rather off our track," admitted Mr. Genocchio. "But then we only do Number Ones. We're opening to-night — just a hall show — at the Casino Bleu."

"It's got very beautiful scenery," continued Julia, who felt that Haute Savoie had not had its full due. "Mountains, and all that. I love scenery."

"So does Ma," said Mr. Genocchio. "Take her out to Richmond and she's happy as a sandboy." He glanced over his shoulder again, evidently reawakening to his present troubles, and was at once beckoned back into the group. Not even the distressing sight

that confronted him, however, could destroy his social sense.

"This is Mrs. Macdermot, Ma. She wondered — "

But Julia had by now realized her error.

"Packett," she corrected firmly.

"Mrs. Packett, Ma." Fred accepted the amendment
without any show of surprise. "She wondered if she
could be of any help."

"No one can help me," moaned Ma in her anguish.
"I wish you'd all go away. I'm dying, and I know it,
and they want to undo me stays."

The five men looked first at each other, then at
Julia. "Women!" that glance seemed to say. *"Women!"*

"Well, they're not going to," said Julia. "The tighter
you are the better, and so I've been telling Mr. Genocchio."

Mr. Genocchio's mother — for such she was — only
moaned again. She was past all comfort, even the
comfort of being let die in her corsets. "Go away!"
she groaned. "Go away and leave me!"

There was evidently nothing to be done. For some
minutes longer they stood sympathetic but impotent,
like bystanders round a fallen horse. Then Fred
slipped his arm through Julia's and drew her quietly
away.

"She's right," he said. "We can't do anything. We'd
better go and get a drink."

— 31 —

### 3

As they settled themselves in the bar Julia, her sympathies still engaged by so much distress, enquired whether the Sixth of the Flying Genocchios was Ma herself.

Fred shook his head.

"No. Ma doesn't fly: my old man was the sixth, and we still keep it on the card. Ma changes the number boards — you know — in tights. And between you and me, she's got past it."

"I don't think they're ever what you'd call becoming," said Julia tactfully. "At least not on a woman. A man with a good figure's different."

"You ought to see our show," said Mr. Genocchio.

With his neat conjurer's movement he produced as though from the air a fan of postcard-size photographs. All except one displayed the Six Flying Genocchios in various astonishing postures — cannoning in mid-air, pendant by the teeth; the card on top was dedicated to Fred alone. And he was superb: in black tights, against a light background, he showed as a long, slim, perfectly balanced triangle, flawlessly tapered from the broad shoulders to the narrow feet. Julia gazed in admiration; she had no need to speak, her eyes were eloquent.

"You'd better come to-night," said Fred earnestly. "What time does your train go?"

"Eleven-forty," said Julia; but she hesitated. That gap of five hours at Paris was already consecrated, in her mind, to her book: she had intended to sit in the First Class waiting-room, lost in a world of literature, while intrigued and intriguing Frenchmen vainly tried to get off with her. That, she felt, was how her journey should begin, for she had already shifted the starting-point to the Gare du Lyon. If she went to a music-hall with the Genocchios, that starting-point would have to be put off still further — till eleven-forty, in fact, which meant so much less time in which to work up her new rôle. Slapdash in everything else — and particularly in affairs of the heart — Julia nevertheless plumed herself on being a conscientious artist; and now these two sides of her character were at their usual game of Devil-pull-Baker. Then she looked at the postcard again, and the Devil won.

"All right," she said. "But I'm not going to miss my train. My daughter will be waiting for me."

His gratitude was cut short by the entrance of the four other Genocchios — three brothers and a cousin — who had followed their leader's example; and in the company of so many males Julia's spirits at once soared. Within five minutes she was the life and soul of the party. The warmth, the rowdiness, the pressure of Fred's knee against her own, all were equally agreeable to her; and only when Fred's hand went under the table as well did she suddenly remember about being a lady. It was hard, too, for those muscular fingers spoke a familiar and exciting language, to which her own cheerful flesh was only too ready to respond; but the spirit triumphed, and Julia rose.

"I'm going to have a look at Ma," she said. "It's too bad, leaving her all alone.

But she only made matters worse. As she went up the companionway a movement of the now pitching boat sent her almost off her feet. Julia staggered back, and but for the strong arm of the trapeze artist would have lost her balance. Fred had followed her up, and was holding her in an embrace so unnecessarily warm as to leave no doubt of his sentiments. He had fallen for her, flat; and Julia, always honest with herself, had no doubt that she could very easily have fallen for him. But she restrained herself nobly; perhaps *The Forsyte Saga,* which she still held under her arm, and which was pressing painfully into her ribs, lent her moral strength. In any case, instead of squeezing Fred back, she drew a little away.

"If you don't behave yourself," she gasped (for the boat was very lively indeed), "I shan't come tonight. I told you before, I'm going out to my daughter."

"All right," said Fred regretfully.

He understood. He was a perfect gentleman. Removing his arm from her waist he gave her no more support (hand under elbow) than the motion of the boat absolutely required. So, decorously, they went up on deck to the chaperonage of Ma.

Julia was sad. She felt that if only things had been different, they could have had a really lovely time.

4

In the Paris train, which was three-parts empty, the Genocchios, with Julia, occupied two adjoining compartments. In the first lay Ma, who after being supported through the Customs had immediately collapsed again, and who was still being ministered to by Joe, Jack, Bob, and Willie; the other, Julia and Fred had all to themselves. This situation was less dangerous than it seemed, for every now and then one of the lesser Genocchios would come in to report progress, or to smoke a cigarette; but even in their solitary interludes Fred's behaviour was now impeccable. He talked quietly and seriously, chiefly about money, and displayed a most becoming family pride. The Genocchios, he would have Julia know, were no mere buskers; Italian by origin, they had come over, if not exactly with the Conqueror, at any rate in the reign

of Charles II. They had play-bills to prove it. There
was a play-bill bearing their name in the Victoria and
Albert Museum. He, Fred, as a nipper, had been taken
to see it by his father and uncle — both notable artists; and it was his own grandfather who had actually
presented it. There wasn't another family in the profession — except, of course, the great Lupinos — who
could show a record to touch it. Julia listened entranced, nor did her interest wane when from the past
Fred worked up to the present. He spoke of money
in the Bank, of a freehold house at Maida Vale; for
in addition to being artists, the Genocchios were also
shrewd. Not one, in two hundred years, had been
buried by the parish. They had had their ups and
downs, of course (and what family hadn't? Look at
the Bourbons!); but for the last century neither a roof
of their own, nor money in the Bank, had ever been
lacking. . . .

"You must make grand husbands," said Julia sincerely.

"We do. And when we marry, we stick. No chop-
ping and changing. Why, Ma wouldn't be with us
now, if Dad hadn't died six months ago. She couldn't
seem to get over it, and then she took a fancy to come
along, and we thought it might brighten her up. But
it was a mistake," finished Fred gloomily. "Her stomach was always a bit weak."

He relapsed into silence, evidently preoccupied with professional troubles. Julia, to distract him, enquired after the rising generation; but his gloom only deepened.

"Bob and Willie are married all right, but they've only a couple of girls between them. Nice bright little kids too, but apart from the name you don't often get a woman acrobat first-class. They're learning dancing." Fred sighed. "I ought to marry myself. But there was a girl, six years ago . . ."

Julia pressed his hand. She couldn't help it, and he took it as meant.

"She fell into the net all right, but something twisted. I think she wished there hadn't been a net. Anyway, she died three months after, and for a bit I hated the whole business."

"I wonder you didn't chuck it," said Julia.

"Chuck it?" He looked at her in surprise. "Of course I didn't chuck it. But it upset me, if you know what I mean. I don't say I've never looked at a woman since, because I have; but marrying 'em was different."

"I don't suppose," said Julia gently, "she'd have wanted you not to . . ."

"She didn't. Just when she was going, she said, 'Give my love to your wife, Fred' — just like that. Here, I didn't mean to upset you!"

For Julia was already weeping. No considerations of

complexion had ever been able to restrain her tender heart, and the tears mingled with her rouge until Fred's handkerchief was patched with pink. When at last she blew her nose she looked five years older, but Fred did not seem to mind. He put one arm about her shoulder and tried to dry her eyes himself.

"No," sobbed Julia. "You go and see to Ma. I want to do my face."

He went at once — the perfect gentleman. Once alone, Julia's tears rapidly ceased, leaving her only pleasantly purged by emotion, and she settled down to her vanity-box with a single mind. There is no doubt that she was enjoying the journey exceedingly: her grief, perfectly genuine while it lasted, was but an extra incident in a thoroughly interesting, variegated trip. She wouldn't have missed it. Even the hasty renovation of her face was amusing to her, and she exchanged her more subdued (or Packett) lipstick for a new Kiss-proof in flamingo red. The effect was striking, but when Mr. Genocchio returned he did not appear to notice it.

"I'm worried about Ma," he said sombrely. "She's still heaving."

Julia looked up with concern.

"And what's more, when she stops heaving, she'll go to sleep. That fool Joe's been filling her up with cognac like pouring it into a flask. If you ask me — "

he flung himself down on the seat — "she'll have to disappoint."

"Well, she's not really part of the show, is she?" asked Julia, in an attempt to console. "I mean, it's not like *you* dropping out."

"She gave us a breather. You can do with a breather in our act. Besides — I know you wouldn't think it to see her now — Ma's good. She's got a good smile, and a sort of way with her. Twinkle in her eye and so on. You'd be surprised the hand she gets."

"It's experience does it," said Julia rather ambiguously. "Can't you get someone at the theatre?"

"We might, but there's not much time, and they hate anyone giving trouble. It's no use worrying. If she's all right she's all right, and if she isn't — "

"If she isn't, I'll have to help you out myself," said Julia.

The words were scarcely past her lips when she knew they were a mistake. There are occasions when one should refrain from well-doing, and this was one of them. When you are going to join your daughter — at any rate, when you are going to join such a daughter as Susan — you shouldn't step aside into borrowed tights. But already Fred was grasping her hands in almost excessive gratitude, and from his fingers into hers ran a peculiar thrill. It was the thrill of theatrical excitement, the thrill of the-other-side-of-the-curtain, to which she had so long been a stranger, and which (as she now realized) she had so sorely missed. "Just this once!" Julia told herself. "Just this one last time, before I'm too old!"

So it was that, instead of going on to the Gare de Lyon, Julia got out at the Gare de Nord.

# Chapter 4

Standing on a chair before the inadequate dressing-room mirror, Julia took a good close-up look at her legs. It was so long since she had seen them in tights that she felt both curious and apprehensive — especially as the tights worn by Ma were definitely out-size. But if Mrs. Genocchio was stout, she was also short, and the material was very elastic. By judicious pulling-up Julia had achieved an adequate degree of tautness, and the reflection in the mirror now set her doubts at rest. Stilted on the two-inch heels of her own silver shoes, Julia's legs rose strong and shapely to the silver loincloth; and if they weren't quite in the mannequin class, they had nevertheless an appeal of their own.

"Men don't care for toothpicks, anyway," said Julia complacently.

With some precaution, on account of her heels, she got down from the chair and took her upper half in turn. It was lightly covered by a sort of bathing-dress top, black like the tights, and a silver bolero. A head-dress composed of black ostrich feathers, springing from a silver tiara, completed the costume; and who-ever designed it (thought Julia) must have had a great deal of taste.

There was a rap at the door; she sprang away from the mirror and took up a nonchalant pose in a good light.

"It's me: Fred," called Mr. Genocchio.

"Come in!" called Julia.

Her heart was suddenly beating fast. Suppose he didn't like her? Suppose he thought her too . . . plump? With passionate repudiation she cast a back-ward glance over all the French pastries she had ever eaten. Why had she eaten them, when she always knew they'd be her ruin? On one occasion, to amuse Mr. Macdermot, she had consumed four éclairs run-ning. . . . "He ought to have been ashamed!" she thought bitterly; and if her agitation seems excessive, it must be remembered that Julia lived ever for the moment, and that this moment was wholly Fred's.

She need not have feared, however. Fred's face, as he stood in the doorway, was positively goopish with admiration.

"You're wonderful," he said at last.

"So are you," said Julia earnestly.

For no photograph could do him justice. A photograph could give only the sheen of his black tights, not the play of muscles beneath; only the statuesque beauty of poise, not the fluid beauty of movement. Fred walked across the room like a black panther; and as she gazed in admiration Julia all unwittingly acquired something she had long coveted. She acquired a scrap of culture, and if she did not recognize it as such, that was because what one looks for among Good Books one does not expect to find in the dressing-room of a music-hall. But so it happened: having filled her eyes with a best in its kind, Julia could not then turn them on a second-best without knowing it for what it was.

"I've too many bits and pieces," she stated, looking at herself in the mirror.

Fred stared in astonishment.

"You're grand. What don't you like?"

"All these." Julia slipped off bolero and headdress and held them behind her back. "They're beautiful, Fred, but I feel I ought to be neater. . . ."

Side by side they gazed at her reflection; but, without the counterbalancing feathers, Julia's hips, emphasized by the silver loincloth, now looked disproportionately large. She shook her head.

"I haven't the figure for it," she admitted sadly. "I'd best leave it alone."

"Your figure's grand," said Fred. And he meant it.

He looked at her with heartfelt admiration. As Julia replaced her headdress he said suddenly, "This place where you're going — is Mr. Packett there too?"

"He's dead," said Julia. "He was killed in the war."

"You must have been an awful kid to get married."

"Sixteen," said Julia. "He was an awful kid to get killed."

"He was a hero all right," said Fred.

Julia nodded without speaking. His sympathy was sweet to her, but she had a suspicion that the spirit of her late husband might not be appreciating it. Sylvester never had liked her friends: when they tried to tell him how brave he was, he used to bite on his thumb and walk away. His shade was probably biting on its thumb now, and Julia, to placate it, hastily changed the subject.

"Isn't it nearly our call, Fred?"

"About four minutes to go. Nervous?"

"Just a bit. It's as soon as I see you bowing?"

"As soon as you see us bowing you come on and change the card — just take the top one off. You can't go wrong if you try."

He grinned at her encouragingly, and Julia suddenly laughed back. For the next hour at least they were bound to each other, they were comrades, they were fellow members of a troupe that was also a family. For the next hour she was to be, not Mrs. Sylvester Packett, but the sixth Flying Genocchio. . . .

"*Allez-oop!*" cried Julia; and the call-boy knocked on the door.

2

Though Julia's legs might not conform to modern mannequin standards, they were greatly to the taste of the patrons of the Casino Bleu. Her second appearance was welcomed with acclamation, and in spite of all resolutions to the contrary she could not help casting a few glad-eyes over the crowded hall. After all, she owed it to Fred to do her best; and her best was very good indeed. There was a bonhomie about her, a willingness to give and receive pleasure, which at once brought her into contact with the audience; and as the turn advanced that contact grew more intimate. Gentlemen here and there shouted personal and appreciative remarks, and Julia's French, though scanty, was sufficient for her to keep her end up. "*Vive la France!*" she called back: "*Vive l'amour! Cherchez la femme* and many of them!" It was not wit, of course, in the classic sense, but it passed for such to her now numerous admirers, and each time she came on the exchanges grew longer and more uproarious. As for Julia, the feel of the boards under her feet, and the smell of a theatre in her nostrils, and the sound

— 45 —

of applause in her ears, all combined to intoxicate her. Like every good actress, she was a little above herself; her personality had swelled to more than life-size; and only a sound professional conscience kept her from stealing the show. The instant she saw the troupe in position she dived for the wings; not till the last wave of applause had ebbed did she reappear. Even so, she felt qualms.

"I can't help it," she murmured to Fred, in a moment when he was not performing. "I know I shouldn't have answered, but I didn't think."

He had no breath to reply — as Julia knew by the superb expansion and contraction of his chest — but his smile said everything. It was all right, he didn't mind; and when at the end of the turn she took her call with the rest his arm slipped through hers and clipped it tight to his side.

"You were grand!" he murmured, while the curtain swung down and up; and at the touch of his cheek, as he whispered, a delicious thrill ran like wine through Julia's body. This, this, she thought, was life! The fouled air was like balmy breezes to her: the people in the audience — good and bad, clean and grimy — were her friends, her kindred, the partakers of her joy. As far as Julia ever felt a communion with nature, she felt it then. And if the nature thus communed with was exclusively human, and therefore (as is commonly believed) less pure, less elevating, than the inanimate, that was the fault of circumstance. The trees and mountains were waiting for her in Savoy.

## 3

Three hundred miles away old Mrs. Packett sat up and looked at the time. It was half-past ten; she had gone to bed too early. Susan always made her grandmother go to bed early when there was to be anything special next day — and then when the next day arrived, made her stay in bed late.

"Silly foolishness!" said old Mrs. Packett aloud. She stretched herself out between the cool, lavender-smelling sheets: her old body felt tough and vigorous — a bit stiff in the joints, but quite capable of sitting up till a reasonable hour. She had been a trifle nervy that afternoon, no doubt; but who wouldn't, with a resurrected daughter-in-law hanging over one's head. Hadn't she a strange young man practically living in the house already? "I didn't come here to entertain a house-party," thought Mrs. Packett crossly; "I came here for rest and peace and Susan's French." But Susan was for once being unreasonable: instead of getting quietly on with her Molière she must needs go and fall in love, and adopt ridiculous martyred attitudes, and write ridiculous letters to a parent she had hardly seen! Mrs. Packett no longer feared Julia; Susan (as no one knew better than her grandmother) was past the malleable stage; but a positive invitation more than any normal woman could resist . . .

"I let Susan domineer," thought Mrs. Packett. "It's a bad habit for both of us." Then, involuntarily, she smiled; Susan's domineering was very sweet. It made one feel — wanted. It kept one up to the mark. Susan was very particular, for example, about her grandmother's hats; she always made straight for the model department, and would look at nothing under two guineas. Once, for a plain black straw with a velvet ruche, she made the old lady pay five. "It's the *line*," Susan had explained. "It makes you look like a Romney." Mrs. Packett always submitted. She still had a tendency to woolly jackets, and to bits of embroidery on the chest, but her hats were admirable. . . .

"Julia never cared," thought Mrs. Packett suddenly. Julia had never cared about anything. A nice girl in her way, most docile and obliging, but always with an air of being only half alive . . . and then she had gone off like that on her own and never come back again! So there must have been something in her, something that Barton was suppressing, was inimical to. Mrs. Packett pondered. In her own youth, before she was married off, she had often thought about living her own life and breeding spaniels: had Julia's thoughts run along the same lines? She never got that husband, it seemed; but what had she done with the seven thousand pounds? Just gone on drawing the income? "If I'd been she," thought Mrs. Packett vigorously, "I'd have started a nice little business." Perhaps Julia had; perhaps she was even now leaving behind a tea-shop, or a hat-shop, or a high-class florist's; and if so, it was to be hoped that she had a manageress she could trust.

Mrs. Packett dozed, stirred, and woke up again. The villa, like the village at its gate, was very still, and through the open window came a gust of sweet pine-scented air.

"A holiday will do her good," thought old Mrs. Packett; for somehow, during her nap, she had become firmly convinced that Julia kept a cake-shop. They would have nice long conversations about it: Julia probably had all sorts of new recipes, and if Anthelmine could be got out of the kitchen, they might even try their hands . . .

"Maids-of-honour," murmured Mrs. Packett; and on that comfortable thought went finally and peacefully to sleep.

4

Meanwhile, in the taxi between the music-hall and the Gare de Lyon, Julia was receiving a proposal of marriage. Ardent yet respectful (Julia indeed keeping him off with an elbow against the chest) Fred Genocchio offered his hand, his heart, his money in the Bank, and his villa at Maida Vale.

"Stay here!" he implored. "Stay here where you belong, Julie, and we'll get married as soon as ever we can. As soon as the week's up the others can go back and we'll have a regular honeymoon. You're the hit of the show, Julie, you're made for it, and I want you so! And you want me, Julie, you know you do!"

She did want him. Her elbow dropped, for a long minute she surrendered to the breath-taking sensation of a trapeze artist's embrace. The motion of the taxi flung them from side to side: first Julia's back, then Fred's, thumped violently against the upholstery; and neither even noticed.

"You'll stay," said Fred.

His voice broke the spell. Julia's eyes opened, travelled vaguely past his shoulder, and focussed at last on two white patches in the darkness. They were the labels on her luggage, whose superscription she had written in London only twenty-four hours earlier: *Les Sapins, Muzin, près de Belley, Ain.*

"I can't!" cried Julia. "I'm going to my daughter!"

She drew herself away and felt Fred stiffen beside her.

"Your daughter doesn't want you like I do!"

"She does, Fred! She's unhappy, and in trouble, and she's there waiting for me! She hasn't wanted me for years — "

"Then she can get along without you now. Julie, my darling — "

"No," said Julia.

Her distress was at least as great as his. To know him suffering, in despair, when with one word she could make all well again, was an agony so acute that she could hardly breathe. It was not her nature to deny: if she took lovers more freely than most women it was largely because she could not bear to see men sad when it was so easy to make them happy. Her sensuousness was half compassion; she could never keep men on a string, which was perhaps why only one had ever married her; and now — the bitterness! — when Fred too wanted to marry her, she had to refuse him. . . .

"Wait!" she pleaded. "Wait till I get back!"

"You won't come back," said Fred sombrely. "They'll get hold of you. That daughter of yours . . ."

Julia felt a sudden chill. Hitherto, unconsciously, she had been limiting that daughter's existence, and her own term of motherhood, to the next month; now she looked into the future. To marry Fred Genocchio would be to give Susan an acrobat for a stepfather. An acrobat among the Packetts! It was unthinkable, and Julia sat thinking of it, silent and in misery, while every jolt of the taxi brought them nearer to the Gare du Lyon.

"There's another thing," said Fred at last. Julia became very still; by the constraint in his voice, by the sudden casualness of his manner, she knew he was about to reveal an inner secret of the heart. "There's another thing," said Fred. "I've never been able — on the high wire — to do a forward somersault. But I've sometimes thought, if I had a son — perhaps *he* might."

5

How Julia got herself into the train, and found her sleeper, and tipped the attendant, she never quite knew. From the moment they left the taxi she had chattered aimlessly, unconscious of what she said, unconscious of Fred's replies, unconscious of everything save the pressure of his arm against her side. But she managed it nevertheless; somehow, suddenly, she was standing in the train corridor, and Fred was on the station platform, and there was a sheet of glass between them. He stood superb and statuesque, moveless as a rock — the best-built man Julia had ever seen. Then the earth seemed to slide under her feet as the train moved out; she waved once, foolishly, then stumbled into her compartment and locked the door.

She was tired as a cat, and no wonder.

She was too tired to cry, certainly too tired to lie awake. After a brief examination of the toilet arrangements — whose novelty and neat commodiousness could not fail to please — Julia hastily creamed her face and got into pyjamas. A couple of darkening bruises, one on each forearm, testified to the uncommon power of Mr. Genocchio's grip. They were the only souvenirs she had of him, and even those would fade. . . .

Julia slid into her bunk and was just preparing for sleep when she noticed a narrow and hitherto unexplored door. Curiosity impelled her to get up and slip back the bolt; she found herself looking not into a cupboard, but into the next (and empty) compartment.

"Handy!" thought Julia.

Then she got back into bed and slept like a log.

# Chapter 5

Ten minutes before the train stopped at Ambérieu
(the time being then twenty-past six) Julia put on her
Matron's Model and stood considering the effect.

It wasn't good. The hat was all right in itself, and
value for money; but it didn't suit Julia. Perhaps the
events of the previous day had left too many traces:
there was a faint old-pro look about her, something
hardy and cheerful, but a trifle worn. . . .

"I need my sleep," thought Julia, tilting the hat
further. It was of fine brown straw, mushroom-shaped,
with a bunch of ribbons in front, but the angle at
which Julia wore it was foreign to its nature. A dowa-
ger at a fête, who had been given champagne instead
of claret-cup, might indeed have achieved the same
effect; only it was not the one Julia sought. She took
the thing off, planted it squarely on her head, and tried
again. Under the straight brim her round black eyes
stared in good-humoured astonishment; the full mouth,
the soft chin, had no business to be there. "You're

right," said Julia to her reflection, "but I'm damn well going to wear it all the same. Don't you know it's the sort of hat she'll be looking for?"

Before the thought of her daughter all else fled. The train was slowing down already; Julia seized her smaller suitcase and hurried into the corridor. She meant to get down the steps at once and be ready on the platform, so that when Susan rushed up there would be no impediment to their embrace — and also so that the label on her suitcase would be properly displayed. For Julia was not relying on filial instinct alone: she had prepared a special piece of cardboard, seven inches by four, with MRS. PACKETT printed in block capitals. Thus not even a stranger could help knowing who she was; and as things turned out — as they so often turned out with Julia — it was a stranger who first addressed her.

"Mees' Packett?"

"Go away," said Julia sharply. He was a very little man, and she looked straight over his head, scanning the platform. No rushing daughterly figure was in sight; the few passengers and their friends were already melting away. Julia was not exactly uneasy, but she could feel uneasiness round the corner. . . .

"Mees' Packett?" implored the man again. "Mees' Packett, Les Sapins, Muzin?" He was holding some-thing out to her, an envelope, which did indeed bear her name; and as Julia looked at it her heart lightened. This time at any rate she knew the hand.

Dear Mother, —

I am so very glad you have come, but I'm not meeting you because six-thirty A.M. at a railway station is such a ghastly place for reunions. The man who gives you this is the station chauffeur, he will bring you to Muzin, and if you like you can have a bath and some more sleep before breakfast.

Affectionately, —

SUSAN.

Julia folded the note away, indicated her luggage to the chauffeur, and followed him out of the station to where the car stood waiting. The freshness of the grey morning air made her shiver: as she powdered her nose again, scrutinizing her features in the little glass, she felt that Susan had perhaps been wise.

"Very sensible indeed," said Julia aloud. To her surprise, she sounded as though she were trying to convince someone. "And very *thoughtful*," added Julia angrily. Then she folded her coat over her knees and appreciated the landscape. Her dominant impression was that it went up. Just for a moment she closed her eyes; and when she reopened them, the car had come to a stop.

## 2

They appeared to be in a farmyard. Poultry fluttered round their wheels, a dog barked, and over the half-door of a stable a horse looked at them intently.

*"Qu'est-ce que c'est?"* called Julia, rapping on the glass.

*"Muzin,"* called back the chauffeur.

Julia looked at the horse, the horse looked at Julia. Directly over its head, fastened to the wall, was a very old sign advertising Singer Sewing Machines.

"Ah!" exclaimed the chauffeur with satisfaction; and leaning from his seat he hailed a group of three men, all bearing agricultural implements, who had suddenly materialized in his path. They wore coloured shirts, blue trousers, and straw hats vaguely moulded in the shape of sun-helmets. These gave them, to Julia's eye, an odd air of tropical explorers; but they were evidently (and on the contrary) natives.

*"Bonjour, messieurs,"* called the chauffeur. *"C'est ici Les Sapins?"*

The eldest of them indicated a narrow opening between two barns. Through there, said the gesture, and up — but up! — one would find Les Sapins. The car moved slowly forward, crawled through the narrows, crossed a square with a fountain in it, and then climbed up — up — by two more lanes (or farmyards) until it

was stopped by a tall iron gate. This the chauffeur
opened; and as its leaves swung apart Julia saw on the
farther side the first stately outposts — huge, dark,
majestic — of an avenue of pines.

She was there.

### 3

The villa of Les Sapins, as originally constructed at
the time of the First Empire, was a small white building partly of two stories, partly of one. It jutted squarely
from the hillside, the upper or front door opening on
a terrace at the foot of the vine, the lower door upon
a terrace over the kitchen-garden. Below were the
dining-room, the kitchen, and the larders; above a
salon and three bedrooms. This accommodation had
sufficed until about 1890, when a new owner of con-
vivial tastes added a billiard-room and two more bed-
chambers. He built straight along on the flat, thus
turning the original square into a rectangle; and besides
elongating the terraces to suit, he joined them by fine
stucco staircases, one at either end of the house. With
the construction of these staircases the glory of Les
Sapins reached its height; and it lasted but two years.
The jovial owner went bankrupt, the villa stood empty,
or was rented and neglected by a succession of summer
tenants; until it finally passed into the hands of an

English spinster named Spencer-Jones, who put in a bath. Miss Spencer-Jones knew Mrs. Packett; and Mrs. Packett took it for the summer of 1936.

Even in decadence, the place was charming. A great Virginia jasmine, dropping red waxen trumpets, concealed the worst deficiencies of the roof. In the deep shadow of the embowering pines the walls still looked white. Tubs of oleander flanked the broken steps, a great lime tree spread shade and perfume over the lower terrace; the rosebushes looked like summerhouses, the summerhouse like a rosebush.

But the glory of the place was the view. From the top of the vineyard, which mounted directly behind the house, one looked straight across a vast circular plain, — mountain-girdled, dotted with villages, varied by little hills, cultivated over every foot, — whose centre was the tiny bishopric of Belley. It was the joke of the village that the back door at Les Sapins was two hundred feet higher than the front; and the pride of the villa that from it one could see Mont Blanc.

4

High up amongst the topmost trees, on the morning of Julia's arrival, stood a tall, fair girl in an old mackintosh. She had been there since six, watching the

Ambérieu road as a beleaguered garrison watches for
the relieving force; yet as the car at last appeared her
expression did not clear. She had called in, not a known
ally, but a strange power. By that impulsive letter,
posted as soon as it was written, she had invited a
stranger to her inmost councils; had tacitly given word
to throw down all defences, expose every weakness,
in return for a reinforcement whose strength she did
not know.

"Have I been a fool?" asked Susan Packett of the
pine trees.

There was naturally no answer. But as the gates
clanged open, as the car nosed up the avenue, Susan
turned her back on the house and began to climb
higher and higher, towards the bare rocks.

# Chapter 6

Under the roses of the porch Julia was received by an elderly Frenchwoman, who at once conducted her into a wide echoing hall. The Frenchwoman, in list-slippers, padded quietly as a cat, but Julia's heels clattered; and it was perhaps then that she received the impression, which never afterwards left her, that she always made twice as much noise as anyone else in the house.

"*La salle de bain,*" said the old woman, proudly flinging open a door.

"*Je vois,*" said Julia; "*très chic.*"

"Madame will take the bath?"

"*Toute de suite,*" agreed Julia. "At any rate, as soon as I've got a sponge out. *Éponge, savon. Dans les valises.*"

"*Madame parle français!*" exclaimed the old woman politely; and a moment later Julia wished she hadn't, for while fetching the bags Claudia let out, in a volley of animated French, what Julia felt sure were mes-

— 61 —

sages from Susan, messages from Mrs. Packett, and general instructions for her own procedure. There was nothing for it, however, but to smile intelligently; and this Julia did.

"*Et — c'est là la chambre de Madame!*" finished the old woman with a flourish.

Julia stood still in the middle of it and looked about her. It was like no room she had ever seen — large, square, with white walls, bare boards, and two windows open on pines, sunshine and a view to a blue hill. There was a white bed in an alcove between two closets, a tiny dressing-table almost concealed behind a great bunch of roses, two chairs, and another table by the windows set with a breakfast-tray and more flowers.

"It's a bit bare," thought Julia, "but there's a lovely lot of room"; and unlocking the larger of her two suitcases she emptied it upon the bed. Her dressing-gown came out at the bottom, but she fished it up, and opened the other case to get her sponge-bag, and moved the roses from the dressing-table to make room for her toilet things. By the time her bath was ready, after only ten minutes' occupation, the whole aspect of the place was so completely altered that even Julia herself felt a slight surprise.

"I've got to be tidy," she warned herself firmly. All ladies were tidy: they had special boxes to pack their shoes in, and special boxes for their gloves, and bags marked "Linen" for their dirty vests. Julia too would have had these things, if finances had permitted; but as they didn't it seemed bootless to worry over details. A broad general effect was (as always) Julia's aim; and this she now achieved by sweeping everything into a closet and shutting the door. But for the roses on the floor, and a stocking on the window-seat, — and some shoes under the table and a powder-box among the breakfast-things, — one would never have known that she had been in the room at all.

## 2

And now, surely, as she lay triumphant in that French bath, was the moment for the Marseillaise. But not a note issued from Julia's throat. She was a little tired after her travelling, and a little sentimental still over Fred; but the chief reason for her silence was that she hadn't yet, so to speak, been introduced. She felt odd enough herself, lying stark naked in a house where she hadn't even met her hostess; how would Susan feel, if after such careful plans for their first meeting her mother prematurely announced her presence by a song from the bath? And since splashing would be almost as bad, Julia found herself moving carefully, almost furtively, in the water: washing her back with precaution, lying down by degrees, so that not a ripple lapped. She found herself pretending, in fact, that she wasn't there; and if she closed her eyes the sensation was remarkably complete. Even the water, unscented, unmoving, didn't feel quite real. It was just a warm atmosphere in which she floated disembodied, no more real than anything else. . . .

"Here!" cried Julia, vaguely alarmed, "I mustn't go to sleep!"

The sound of her own voice aroused her; she at once sat up, listening intently, to see whether anyone else had been aroused as well. But all was quiet, and with a sigh of relief she climbed unobtrusively out and began to dry. There were two bath-towels, beautifully large and white, besides a smaller one of linen, with embroidery on the edge; and though it was impossible to make real use of the lot, Julia had such a damn good try that she heard the maid's slippered feet in the passage, and her own door open and shut, while she was still polishing up her thighs.

"It's my breakfast," thought Julia; and, anxious to be in the right place at the right time, — another form of self-effacement, — she hurried on her clothes and hastened back to her room. There was no one there, but rolls and honey had appeared on the breakfast-table; anxious to be found in the right garments, Julia exchanged her dressing-gown for a white piqué frock and hastily powdered her nose. And it was a mercy she did so, for the next moment there was a rap at the door, and behind the door was a coffeepot, and carrying the coffeepot was her daughter Susan.

### 3

At the first sight of her Julia's heart leapt up. For Susan was pretty, and pretty in a peculiarly ladylike way. She had the Packett height and slimness, the fair Packett hair, and eyes of that rare clear grey that is unflecked, unshaded, by any tint of blue. There was nothing of Julia in that face, and nothing of Julia in the sweet virginal voice.

"Good morning," said Susan.

She was still holding the coffeepot (could it be protectively?) so that Julia, poised for an embrace, had to sink as it were back into herself before answering.

"Good morning," she said, trying to keep the quiver out of her voice. "Good morning, Susan."

The girl set down the pot (could it be that she felt the danger pass?) and smiled gravely.

"Yes," she said. "I'm Susan. I hope you didn't mind my not coming to meet you. But — "

"But it's so much nicer here," finished Julia quickly.

"It shocked Grandmother, but I thought you'd understand." (That was heartening, at any rate!) "And

she's also rather shocked," continued Susan, smiling
again, "because I wouldn't let her get up to welcome
you. She's sitting up in bed now, waiting for the moment you've finished your breakfast. But I had to have
you to myself first."

Such pleasant words, spoken in so grave and charming a voice, filled Julia with maternal joy. But it was
a joy still a little constrained: as she sat down to the
table, and let Susan pour out for her, the odd feeling
of the bathroom surged over her once again. Was this
truly her daughter, standing so dutifully over the
breakfast-tray? Was this strange bare house one in
which she herself had truly a daughter's rights? It
didn't feel real. Nothing felt real, not even the bread
between her teeth, which she had to make an effort
to swallow. . . .

"Are you feeling shy?" asked Susan unexpectedly.
"I am."

Julia beamed.

"Till you said that I was." Impulsively she got up
from the table; but she was still too shy to give her
daughter a kiss. Susan, in spite of so much charm,
didn't look the kissing sort; and as the thought crossed
her mind Julia felt an added curiosity to hear about
Susan's young man. "Tell me all about him!" cried
Julia impetuously; and sat down on the window-seat
with ears and heart open.

Susan, however, had her own plans. She smiled affectionately, but with a shake of the head.

"His name is Bryan Relton, he's twenty-six and a barrister, and he'll be quite well off. You'll see him at lunch. Only it's no use discussing anything now, is it? I mean until you've got to know us both, it's not fair to ask for your opinion."

Nicely put, thought Julia; but she knew what it meant all the same. "Not fair" meant "no use"; and though the assumption was perfectly sound, such rationality, in a girl in love, struck her as exaggerated. Or was it rather caution? Was Bryan Relton one of those young men for whom nothing much can be said, but who have only to make a personal appearance to carry all before them? So wondered Julia, but not for long; she was too much occupied with observing her daughter. The more you looked at her — and Susan was now sitting close on the window-seat — the more perfect you saw she was. Her beautiful small ears lay flat to her head; her beautiful small hands, brown but perfectly kept, sprang delicately from the wrists as leaves from the slender stem. And then she was so clean! Julia was clean herself, she had a bath every day, so long as there was gas: but Susan's was the cleanliness of a running stream — something as much and as essential a part of her as her height or her grey eyes.

"I don't wonder he's wild about her," thought Julia, returning, though only in silence, to the forbidden topic. "I expect he's poetical." She pictured him tall and thin and very serious — the sort that adores once and for a lifetime; and she also pictured him a good deal older than his years, since it is generally to men above thirty that the virginal makes most appeal. "I bet he thinks she's a sort of angel," mused Julia, highly approving. . . .

"What would you like me to call you?" asked Susan suddenly. "You look so young to be called 'Mother.'"

Julia felt a pang of disappointment. Of course she wanted to be called "Mother" — hadn't she come all the way from England for that very purpose? She wanted to be called "Mother," "Mumsie," "Mummy," "Mum"; but from Susan's tone she knew at once that none of these vocables would ever find favour. As before, it was nicely put; but behind the tribute to her appearance Julia divined a shrinking, an embarrassment, which her own warm heart found difficult to comprehend.

Instead of directly answering, she said, a little wistfully, "You can't think how glad I was to get your letter. I know I've never been as much to you as I should — that was my own fault; and it made me so happy that you should still turn to me. I know I'm not really your sort — "

She broke off, for her daughter's embarrassment was now unconcealed. Susan had got up and was staring fixedly out of the window.

"I think you were perfectly right," she said rapidly. "You wanted to live your own life, and you did. I've no patience with people who sacrifice themselves to other people's ideas. If you want to know, I've always admired you."

"You — you have been happy with them?" asked Julia anxiously.

"Perfectly happy. Grandmother's an absolute darling, and so was Grandpa. And, I can't help knowing it, I've made them happy too. I've somehow consoled them for losing my father." She turned back, her face eager. "Will you tell me all about him, please?"

The moment had come — the moment for intimacy, for the long mother-and-daughter talk to which Julia had so much looked forward. But her heart, instead of leaping, sank within her. For when it came to the point — when the image of Sylvester Packett should have sprung fully-formed in her mind — she found she remembered practically nothing about him at all.

4

"He was a first lieutenant in the Gunners — " began Julia carefully; and paused. There had been so many first lieutenants, a lot of them in the Gunners, and they had all been very much alike. Young, tired, reckless in gaiety, but never — never quite all there. Never completely with you, as though they had all left part of themselves somewhere else. You could be out dining with a man, having a perfectly lovely time, and suddenly across the room he would catch another man's eye, or a man would pause by your table, and all at once they were somewhere else and you were left behind. It had seemed as if war were a sort of fourth dimension, into which they slipped back without noticing, even out of your arms. . . . So you never really knew them — at least the Julias didn't — and how could you remember anyone you hadn't properly known?

"Don't, if it hurts you," said Susan gently.

In spite of her self-justification, Julia felt ashamed. She cudgelled her brains.

"He liked the Piccadilly better than Murray's," she said at last. "Most of them didn't. But then he wasn't like the rest in lots of ways."

"No?" prompted Susan.

"He was very serious. And he had very good manners. He was so good to me —" Julia broke off: impossible to tell his daughter exactly *how* good! And overcome by the effort, and by self-reproach, and by easy yet sincere regrets, she accidentally did the only right thing. She put down her head and burst into tears.

"Oh, don't!" cried Susan remorsefully. "Please, *please!*"

But Julia wept on. She might forget Sylvester for years on end, but when she did think about him it was properly. He was the best man she had ever known, he had taken thought for her, he had left her his name and — had she wished for it — the protection of his home. He had married her! No one else . . .

"Except Fred," thought Julia.

The events of the previous evening — at the Casino Bleu, in the taxi going to the station — rose incongruously in her mind. She thrust them back, but not before they had given her, oddly enough, something she wanted.

"I've remembered another thing," she sobbed. "Something that was really *him*. Whenever he was upset, he used to bite his thumb. Not the nail, you know, but down by the joint."

With a quick movement Susan stood up.

"You'd like to go in the garden," she said abruptly. "No — you'd like to see Grandmother. I'll see — I'll tell her. It's lovely in the garden. I'll tell you when Grandmother — "

Her lips trembled, she seemed to be speaking at

random. Suddenly she spread out her hands and looked at them with a kind of awe.

"They got *me* out of it when I was ten," she said; and went quickly from the room.

# Chapter 7

Julia did as she was bid. When she had made up her face — and it needed it badly — she went out by the porch, and down the broken flight of steps, and so found herself on the lower terrace. She had no impulse to explore: her instinct bade her keep close to the house; and a chair under the lime tree at once attracted her eye. It was very comfortable, and by pulling it forward she could rest her feet on the low stone wall. Emotion did not as a rule tire her — it bucked her up; but the emotion of the last hour was different. It had been constrained, not expansive. . . .

"I'm a fool!" Julia told herself sharply. "Did I expect her to fall on my neck?"

The truth was that she had so expected. After that letter, after her own swift response, the actual meeting with Susan had been an anticlimax. There had been tears, indeed, but tears of the wrong sort; and none shed by Susan. "She doesn't cry easily," thought

Julia. "She'd never cry before a stranger. . . ." There was the rub: that Julia, who could get intimate with a trapeze artist after five minutes' conversation — who was intimate with a salesman after buying a pair of shoes — had talked for an hour to her own daughter, about the girl's own father and lover, without the least intimacy at all.

"I'm a fool," thought Julia again. "It's just because she's such a perfect lady. And what *I* need is a good sleep."

She did not sleep then, but the quiet of the morning, the sunshine, the warm odours that rose from the kitchen-garden below, gradually soothed and raised her spirits. From where she sat she could see no further than the roofs of the village: she was in a little tree-encircled world, strange but delightful in its picturesqueness. A lovely world! Julia had no eye for detail; she could appreciate only such obvious effects as the bright clear green of the tree-tops, the flaming mass of the jasmine against a white wall; but what she enjoyed she enjoyed thoroughly. She liked the oleanders — the pink ones better than the white; she admired the showy intention of the broken staircase; and it also struck her that her own white figure, against the dark blue cushions of her chair, must be making a very pleasant effect.

Here Julia paused. Beneath the agreeable surface

of her thought stirred the consciousness of something lacking. What was it? She was very comfortable, she had ceased to worry about Susan, yet that wasn't enough. She wanted something more. What was it?

"Of course!" thought Julia, surprised at her own obtuseness.

There ought to be a man there. There ought to be a man to enjoy her white frock, to admire her sensibility when she pointed out the jasmine. It wasn't because she, Julia, couldn't do without one. She didn't want a man *personally,* but because in that lovely place — with its roses and terraces and no doubt lots of little hidden nooks — the lack of one seemed such a waste.

At that moment, a man appeared.

2

Julia admired him greatly. He was young, deeply sunburnt, and dressed in a blue shirt, tan-coloured trousers, and sandalettes that had once been white. Over his shoulder was slung a light jacket, on his head he wore one of the coarse straw hats, shaped like sun-helmets, which Julia had noticed in the village. This, as he approached, he respectfully doffed.

*"Bonjour, Madame!"*

Julia nodded affably. She hoped he was a gardener, for though obviously not a man to sit on the terrace with, she felt he would be nice to have about. He could carry cushions for her, light her cigarette; perhaps pick for her, and shyly present, bouquets of wild flowers. . . .

"*Bonjour, mon homme,*" returned Julia graciously.

The young man grinned. The change was so sudden — the flash of white teeth so altered, while illuminating, his countenance — that Julia received quite a shock. Though the hat was still in his hand, he now looked scarcely respectful at all: his regard was frankly admiring. He looked her over, evidently liked what he saw, and gave her what was practically a glad-eye. The French were like that, Julia knew, and one had to make allowances; but in a gardener it was — well, unsuitable.

"Go and get on with your work!" she said sharply. "*Allez-vous en!*"

He went at once (but apparently unabashed) towards the kitchen-garden gate; and in spite of her disapproval Julia could not help acknowledging that his figure, in its gay foreign clothes, lent a touch of picturesque interest to the landscape. Though not tall, he was very athletic: when he reached the gate he did not open it, but vaulted over. Julia heard his voice uplifted in French, apparently addressing one of the maidservants; a woman called back, a dog barked, and then all was still again.

"I bet he's a terror in the village," thought Julia.

The incident had quite woken her up, and she had just decided to go for a walk round the house when Susan reappeared at the other end of the terrace. Julia went towards her, and when they had met — not calling out, vulgarly, from a distance — Susan gave her message.

"Would you like to come and see Grandmother? I'm afraid I've been a long time, but she'd gone to sleep again."

"I nearly slept, myself," said Julia, as they walked up the steps. "It's so lovely and peaceful."

"I do hope you won't be bored here," said Susan.

"I'm never bored where there's scenery," returned Julia grandly. "I just love a nice view."

Susan smiled, but did not look particularly reassured. "Grandmother's room has the best view of any," was all she said; and opening the door she ushered Julia in.

### 3

Mrs. Packett was sitting in bed wearing a very smart boudoir-cap and a woollen cardigan. She smiled as Julia came in, and held out her hand; but she also had a complaint to make, and with the frank egoism of age at once made it.

"I have been to sleep again," she announced severely. "Of course I go to sleep if Susan forces me to have breakfast in bed. It's very bad for me, and there are crumbs among the clothes."

"You'll be up in ten minutes," said Susan consolingly. "Claudia's seeing to your bath now."

"I wanted to get up *early*," insisted Mrs. Packett. "I wanted to be up to meet you, Julia, but Susan wouldn't let me. She's not going to let me lunch with you either, because — "

"Grandmother!"

"Go away, Susan." Mrs. Packett watched her granddaughter out of the room and went on where she had left off. " — Because she wants to put this young man through his paces all by herself. I'm supposed to be a disturbing influence — like in table-turning. As you'll very soon find out, my dear, Susan does anything she likes with me."

Julia smiled.

"Not altogether. You know why *I*'m here?"

"Of course I do, and I'm very glad. Draw that curtain back and let me have a look at you."

Julia did as she was told and let in a burst of sunlight not only on herself but also upon Mrs. Packett. The old woman stood it well; her plump weather-

browned face was fresh and lively, her small grey eyes
looked interestedly on the world. Age suited her. As a
girl she must have been pretty; in middle life, as Julia
remembered her at Barton, she was scarcely distinguish-
able against the general background of well-bred dowdiness; now she had emerged again, complete and
individual, with her prejudices elevated to principles
and her dowdiness ripened into distinction. "She's
*tough*," thought Julia admiringly. . . .

"You've put on weight," remarked Mrs. Packett.
"But you look well. What have you been doing with
yourself all this time?"

Julia paused. The figure of Mr. Macdermot (and of
many another) passed rapidly before her inward eye.
The day at Elstree when she fell into the fountain (five
times in three hours) was fresh in her memory. So
were several other episodes, all as poignant and interesting at the time as they were now unsuitable for
relation.

"Nothing much," she said. "I've just been living in
town."

"You don't keep a cake-shop?"

"A cake-shop?" Julia was surprised. "I've never
thought of it."

"I have," said Mrs. Packett energetically. "I was
thinking of it only last night. It would just suit you —
and you've got the capital."

Here was some of the thin ice Julia had been dreading. She cut a daring figure on it.

"Suppose I lost the lot?"

"You wouldn't, if you had any sense. Everyone I know in London complains that they can never get a homemade cake. I could give you twenty addresses now. I'd write to them all personally. And if you like, while you're here, I'll show you my special maids-of-honour."

Julia listened to these plans with astonishment: she had never credited her mother-in-law with so much enterprise. But a topic involving capital was not, in her opinion, one to be too closely pursued.

"I'll think about it," she said. "At the moment I can't think of anything but Susan. I'm afraid you'll feel I've come to interfere."

"Of course you have," said Mrs. Packett. "Not that I blame you. Nor do I blame Susan, though I think she's behaving most unreasonably. I expect you thought she was locked in her room on bread and water?"

"I expected to find her . . . worse," Julia admitted.

"Instead of which I'm feeding them both twice a day on the fat of the land. You'll see at lunchtime. You'll see *him*. Susan made me promise not to speak about him until you'd met, in case I prejudiced you; but you know I disapprove, because she must have said so in her letter. Isn't that so?"

"Yes," agreed Julia, "but she didn't say why."

Mrs. Packett looked surprised: "Simply because she's too young. I've nothing against Bryan personally. But no girl should get married at twenty."

"Then you don't object to an engagement?"

"Until Susan is twenty-one I do. If they would like to announce their engagement next year, and get married when Susan is twenty-three, I have no objection at all."

This was a new light on the subject, and Julia considered it thoughtfully. Susan's birthday was in March — only eight months away — and after a formal engagement the time of waiting could probably be abridged. Then why wouldn't Susan wait? Why so desperate a measure as the fetching of her mother from London? She wasn't — Julia could have sworn it — consumed by the impatience of passion. She was escaping from no present ills. Then why . . . ?

"I can't understand it," said Mrs. Packett, meeting her thought. "She's enjoying the life at Girton, she loves it. Another two years, and one getting ready, shouldn't seem long to her. And at the beginning she agreed with me; it's only in the last few weeks that she's become so — so heady."

"And the young man?" asked Julia. "Is he willing to wait too?"

"If he is, my dear, he can hardly say so, with Susan

clamouring to get married next month." Mrs. Packett sighed. "Perhaps I'm being selfish. Perhaps, when I say I want her to have her girlhood, I really mean I want to keep her a little longer for myself. You know, my dear, we've always been very grateful to you?"

Julia moved uneasily. What a family they were for distributing nonexistent virtues!

"I'm grateful to *you*," she said almost curtly. "When I see Susan now I know I could never have done half as well for her. She's her father's daughter much more than mine — and a very good thing too."

The old woman's glance was suddenly so shrewd that Julia was taken by surprise. "I bet it was she who wouldn't let Sue come and stay with me!" she thought. And quite right, all things considered: there were some people who shouldn't mix, however nearly they were related; the tie of the spirit was closer than the tie of the flesh, and in spirit Susan was pure Packett. Julia's spirit — "If I've got one!" she thought suddenly. "If you ask me, I'm all flesh!"

Mrs. Packett put out her hard old hand and touched Julia's plump one.

"You're my daughter-in-law, and I'm very glad to see you. Stay with us as long as you can."

"I'll stay for always!" cried Julia impetuously; but they were both wise enough to take the sentiment at its true value.

# Chapter 8

The dining-room at the villa was a small square apartment, always rather dark because of the great jasmine, whose lower garlands drooped over its French window like a natural sun-blind. The light that filtered through was green rather than golden, and Julia, putting her head in from the bright terrace, could at first make out no more than the round table with its white cloth. She had no real business there, but she was hungry and wanted to see how lunch was getting on. The sight of cutlery and glass, laid for three, encouraged her, and so did the carafe of wine. She wouldn't have said "No" to a cocktail, but the opportunity, if Barton habits still prevailed, was not likely to arise.

"I must just learn to do without them," thought Julia, as she returned to the seats under the lime tree. "They're rotten for the complexion, and it's a bad example for Susan. Besides, anyone who knows about

wine says they're absolute muck. . . . If I could have
one, I'd have a Manhattan."

With an effort she wrenched her thoughts away
and directed them to the surprising metamorphosis of
Mrs. Packett. The old lady's vigour had made a deep
impression on her. "She wasn't like that at Barton,"
reflected Julia, wondering. "If she'd wanted me to
start a cake-shop then, I might have done it." Or had
Mrs. Packett even then hankered after commercial
enterprise, and had she, Julia, been too much wrapped
up in her own misery, too unresponsive to all outside
impressions, to notice? Julia thought not. It seemed
to her more likely that her mother-in-law was of the
type, not rare among Englishwomen, in whom full
individuality blossoms only with age: one of those
who, at sixty-one, suddenly startle their relatives by
going up in aeroplanes or by marrying their chauf-
feurs. . . .

"Well?" said the voice of Susan. "How do you think
Grandmother is looking?"

"Splendid," said Julia promptly. "Has she been up
in an aeroplane?"

Susan looked surprised: "No, she hasn't. But she did
talk — how odd! — of flying to Paris. I thought it might
be too much for her."

"You'll have a job to stop her flying back," prophesied Julia, tucking in her feet so that Susan could pass

to the second chair. But Susan did not move. She hadn't come out to talk about her grandmother.

"Lunch is just ready," she said. "And — he's here."

Julia preceded her into the dining-room and saw a young man, deeply sunburnt, who greeted her with a cheerful smile. He wore a blue shirt, tan-coloured trousers, and sandalettes which had once been white.

2

"This is Bryan Relton — my mother," said Susan from the doorway.

His smile broadened to a grin.

*"Bonjour, Madame!"*

"Well, I'm damned!" thought Julia. But there was no time to marvel. Her surprise had been patent, but she made a good come-back.

*"Bonjour, mon homme,"* said Julia blandly. "We've met before, Susan, and I thought he was the gardener."

Susan joined in their laughter, but she was not quite pleased. Bryan was her property, her surprise: she was like a child who has hidden a puppy in the tool-shed, and then finds it gambolling with the grown-ups. The grown-ups couldn't help it, but it was tactless of the puppy to get out. . . .

"It's those clothes," she said, with a humorous lift of the eyebrows.

— 85 —

"Practical, cheap, and picturesque," retorted the young man. "Don't they suit the landscape better, Mrs. Packett, than a gent's summer suiting?"

"Very much better indeed," said Julia. "And if you think you're going to make a fool of me," she added mentally, "you'll have to think again."

They sat down and ate home-grown hors d'œuvres — eggs and radishes, chopped onion, beans in a vinaigrette sauce. The food was excellent, the meal proceeded pleasantly; Susan described the beauties of the neighbourhood, Julia (with expurgation) the incidents of her voyage. The lacunae were necessarily so great that there was practically nothing left to her save the state of the Channel, the emptiness of the Paris train, and the convenience of the *wagon-lit;* but to Susan at least such uneventful voyaging seemed perfectly natural. Of Bryan, Julia was less sure.

"Poor Mrs. Packett!" he said. "Didn't you find a soul to speak to?"

"There was quite a nice woman on board — a schoolmistress, I think," said Julia.

"Very informative," said Bryan respectfully. That was the trouble — he was too respectful by half. He aroused Julia's suspicions; and as luncheon proceeded, so those suspicions increased. In talking to Susan he seemed perfectly natural — affectionate, admiring, anxious to please; whenever he spoke to Julia, and however deferential the words, there was what could only be described as a look in his eye.

"I do so love the country!" announced Julia with enthusiasm.

"I'm *sure* you do," agreed Bryan warmly. But the look in his eye said — well, it practically said: "Garn!"

As for Susan, though her gaze turned constantly from her lover's to her mother's face, she appeared to see nothing of their intercourse save its pleasant surface. Perhaps that underrunning current was something you couldn't see unless you could recognize it: the tacit intimacy of two complete strangers who came — how to put it? — out of the same box.

And as her suspicions thus crystallized, Julia felt a pang of sheer dismay.

"I believe he's the same sort as I am!" she thought. "Now what the hell am I to do?"


### 3

The first thing, obviously, was to find out more. It was possible that she had been mistaken; but if so, then for the first time in her life her surest instinct had let her down. It had always been her great asset — often her only asset — that she could tell at sight who was her sort and who wasn't: which of two men at a bar, for example, would stand her a dinner, which of two women in a ladies' room would put her up for the night. On such knowledge as this, indeed, Julia's dinners and beds had often depended; her highly successful partnership with Mr. Macdermot had sprung from a single glance exchanged in a railway-train. No speech was possible, the compartment being full; but Julia had been absolutely certain that if she kept close to him at the station something would happen. And it did happen: "Like a lift?" said Mr. Macdermot, as they passed the taxi-rank; "I don't mind if I do," said Julia; and after that they were together for four years.

"That's no reason why I shouldn't be wrong this time," thought Julia stubbornly; but her daughter's answer, when later that afternoon she enquired where Susan and Mr. Relton had first met, struck her as a bad omen.

"In a train," said Susan.

She spoke calmly and distinctly — so very calmly, with such super-distinctness, that even Julia, who, apart from Mr. Macdermot, had been meeting people in public conveyances all her life — even Julia noticed the effort. Those three words were evidently regarded by Susan as a fence to be taken; with the courage and composure of a gentlewoman she had set her teeth and taken it. But Julia's calm, as she continued, was merely natural.

"How long ago?"

"About six weeks. It was between Strasbourg and Paris, when I was meeting Grandmother before we came on here. He helped me about my baggage, and we had lunch together. You know how it is when you're travelling."

Her mother nodded. The image of Fred Genocchio waved to her from the Gare du Lyon, and in her heart Julia waved back. That was travelling — to knock up against strange men, and leave a little of your heart with them, and receive a scrap of theirs in return, and then go on with your memory by so much enriched and your forearms (if the stranger happened to be a trapeze-artist) blue with bruises.

"And then," supplied Julia encouragingly, "he asked for your address?"

"No!" said Susan. "Of course he didn't. But we were talking about France, and the various parts, and I mentioned Muzin. And then a week later — he turned up here."

Julia looked at her daughter with interest. The ice had thawed: Susan was in a positive glow. "How pretty she is!" thought Julia; and it seemed wonderful to her that so slight a cause should have produced so great an effect. But no doubt to a young girl like Susan the adventure had been both romantic and remark-able in the extreme — enough to make her fall in love

with anybody. And the young man was attractive as
well. That sort was, mused Julia unkindly.

Aloud she said, "He's been here nearly five weeks,
then? Hasn't he anything to do?"

"He's a barrister," said Susan quickly. "They can
take long holidays. And this is a special one, before
he really settles down to work. It's doing him so much
good!"

"Where is he staying?"

"At the lodge. At least, it isn't really our lodge,
it's let out, with the vine. But Grandmother arranged it."

"Your grandmother?" said Julia, startled. "I suppose she wanted to know all about him?"

Susan glowed again.

"That's the wonderful part. She *did* know. Bryan's
father — Sir James — used to know Grandfather. He
actually came to Barton once. It's years and years ago,
almost before the War; but Grandmother remembers
him perfectly."

Julia opened her mouth and shut it again. Oddly
enough, she remembered Sir James too.


4

Her recollection of him was very clear indeed.
Without even closing her eyes she could see a dressing-

room at the Frivolity — the cramped, old-fashioned sort, rather dirty — six girls in various stages of pleasing disarray, and on the one sofa a large recumbent figure. The figure was that of Sir James. The six girls were discussing whether to get someone to chuck him out, or to let him sleep it off. Julia, always kind-hearted, had been for the second course: she had rashly guaranteed that if they left him there during the last part of the show he would be able at the end of it to leave under his own power. And then over the senseless form an argument arose: Julia, said one of the girls, was notoriously maternal; but where would *they* all be if his wallet was missing? Whereupon Julia, with a fortunate blow, laid the girl out upon Sir James's chest. An animated scene indeed! . . . And so different from the one immediately before her eyes that Julia felt a momentary doubt of her own identity. Could she really have taken part in that rowdy passage? And yet if she tried she could still feel, pressing against her ears, the cardboard bananas of her vegetable headdress. The girls had been — for some long-forgotten theatrical reason — the dessert: her opponent wore grapes, piled high in a basket, and very fragile. . . .

The curious thing was that Sir James never woke. He simply put up an arm and drew his unexpected bedmate into a more comfortable position. He also (still in his sleep) addressed her as "Wendy": and since this happened to be the name of the leading lady, recrimination soon gave way to happy conjecture. They were twenty seconds late for their call, and got no end of a blowing-up about it. . . .

It will thus be seen that Julia had every reason for changing her mind and shutting her mouth. She had also a good deal to think about. If there was anything in heredity, it seemed to her, considerable light was thrown upon the young Bryan's conduct — and a light in which that conduct assumed other and less fair hues than those distinguished by Susan. All that family, thought Julia — perhaps unfairly — were born pursuers. If Bryan had met Susan in a country drawing-room, and been invited to call afterwards, he would probably have lost all interest; but to meet her in a train, to see her vanish into the blue just as he had begun to get going — that was very different! Circumstance, by supplying the coquetry Susan lacked, had made her desirable.

"I want you to get to know him," Susan was saying earnestly. "I want you to talk to him by himself. You'll carry so much more weight with Grandmother than I can, because she thinks you're more experienced."

Julia's tenderness, as she looked at her daughter, was not unmixed with irritation.

"It's just possible that I am," she said. "You can't learn without living."

"But some things you don't need to learn," said Susan steadily. "You *know*. Will you talk to Bryan if I fetch him now? He's in the vine."

Julia nodded. It was plain that the day had already been mapped out for her — for her, and for everyone else in the Villa des Sapins. Bryan awaited his cue in the vine, Mrs. Packett lunched alone in the billiard-room, exactly as Susan bade them. Only Susan herself seemed to have freedom of movement; and she now used it to bring the most important of her puppets from the wings and plant him firmly in the centre of the stage.

"Enter Juvenile Lead," thought Julia, as she watched Bryan come down the staircase alone. Her own rôle being merely that of confidante, she sacrificed elegance to comfort and put her feet up on the low wall.

### 5

Armed with her private information, Julia entered on the engagement with a good deal of confidence. Nor did the young man, as he deferentially took his seat beside her, seem at all uneasy. "He's got all his father's cheek!" thought Julia; and a moment after was shocked by her unfairness. Why shouldn't the

boy be easy, when his conscience was clear? Weren't
his intentions honourable? Didn't he want to marry
Susan? "I can't help it, I know his sort," thought
Julia vaguely, and thus, though she did not then pur-
sue it, again touched the clue to her distrust. Bryan
was waiting for her to begin.

"I'm going to ask a lot of impertinent questions,"
said Julia amiably.

The young man's attitude became if possible more
deferential than before. It was almost too deferential
to be true.

"I'll supply anything you like, Mrs. Packett, from a
birth certificate to a banker's reference."

"That's not quite what I mean," said Julia. "I can
leave all that to Sue's guardians. But, to begin with,
when you met Susan — where were you going?"

"To Paris."

"How long had you been in Strasbourg?"

"A couple of days."

"You'd gone straight there from England? You
hadn't got off at Paris, for instance?"

"Certainly not," said the young man virtuously. "I
went straight as a die."

"Well, it's a long way to go for two days," said
Julia. "*Why* did you go there?"

"To visit friends."

"A girl?"

"As a matter of fact — yes."

"And she was otherwise occupied, so you came back," elaborated Julia.

The young man looked at her with interest.

"See here, darling — " ("That's more his style!" thought Julia) — "all that may be just as you say, but it has nothing to do with Susan."

"It may or it mayn't," said Julia. "I'm just establishing the facts. Were you going to stay in Paris or move on?"

"I hadn't decided. I never make plans when I'm on holiday."

"I can understand that," said Julia thoughtfully, "because I'm just the same. I like to see what turns up."

There was a long pause while old Mrs. Packett, walking slowly through the heat, passed from the shadow of the house to the shadow of the pines. Even in her unsuitable black gown, and her woolly jacket, she looked so perfectly the lady that Julia was forced to spare her a moment's attention.

"All right," said Bryan suddenly. "I *was* at a loose end. But once I got here — if you think I'm just after a holiday affair — "

"No," agreed Julia. "This house — and the people in it — aren't conducive to holiday affairs. I just wanted to know how you got here at all."

She stood up, smiled pleasantly, and left him. She had given him something to think about, and she had played confidante long enough. But even so, she did not have the last word. The last word, though unspoken, was Bryan Relton's.

"If it comes to that," said his look, "how the hell did *you?*"

# Chapter 9

How indeed? wondered Julia, first with apprehension, then, as the days went by, with a secret and amused surprise. For she was getting away with it: that perfectly ordered house, that little world of perfectly bred people, accepted her as a natural inhabitant. She felt rather as a bystander might feel who, inadvertently swept off the curb into some royal procession, nevertheless manages to hold his own between the Ambassador on one side and the Admiral on the other. She had to try hard, of course; she never drank with her mouth full, and never sang in the bath, and always discussed impersonal subjects in a low, ladylike voice. And there were naturally some bad moments: there was that terrible morning, for instance, when Claudia the maid spilt a bottle of scent, and she, Julia, had said what she thought of her; the woman didn't really mind — anyway, she didn't understand half of it — but Susan's face as she paused by the open door! It had been a white mask of distaste, before which Julia and the maid equally shrank. Julia — the maid on one side, Susan on the other, the unfortunate bystander — had dropped an *h*. And then the scent itself, though expensive, had been far from a success: the night Julia wore it at dinner Susan, on some perfectly courteous pretext, got up and opened another window. . . .

If Mrs. Packett was the Ambassador and Bryan Relton the Admiral, Susan was a Bishop, walking just in front, and now and then turning back with suspicious looks. But by stepping carefully (and avoiding the Admiral's eye) Julia nevertheless hoped to hold her own.

2

The village of Muzin was tiny — so tiny that it had neither church nor schoolhouse of its own. It had not even a post office. To buy stamps, and to receive religious or secular instruction, its inhabitants had to walk a mile and a half to the bigger village of Magnieu. Belley, with its shops and market, its cathedral and promenade, lay even farther — nearly four miles off, along a road for the most part unshaded; so that the occupants of the villa were almost completely cut off from the outside world. Twice a week, however, a hired car carried them into the metropolis for purposes of shopping, and on these occasions Susan, armed with a list from Anthelmine the cook, would exercise her beautiful French on the admiring tradesmen. Everyone from the villa accompanied her as a matter of course, and on the second morning after her arrival Julia, warned at breakfast of the approaching excursion, was ready in her hat a quarter of an hour too soon.

"All agog?" asked Bryan, joining her on the porch.

"I hate unpunctuality," explained Julia. "I think it's so rude."

"Rude but natural," supplemented Bryan. "Like so much else. What are you going to do at Belley? Shop with Susan or come pub-crawling with me?"

"Or if you like old buildings," said Susan from the front door, "there's the cathedral — not very interesting — and a rather charming close, and one of the old gates. Grandmother doesn't walk much, but I'd love to show you them."

Julia withered Bryan with a glance. Pub-crawling, indeed, when there was a cathedral to be looked at!

"I'll come too," he said at once. "I'm good on architecture."

"You're not and you won't," retorted Susan. "We'll meet you at the Pernollet. Grandmother's taking us all there for lunch."

"Alleluia," said Bryan simply.

### 3

The Pernollet, as becomes a restaurant with a monument to Brillat-Savarin not a stone's throw from its door, is a very good restaurant indeed. It is better, in its kind, than the cathedral, or the close, or the old gateway, so that Julia had perhaps some excuse for preferring it to all three. The hour spent looking at architecture with Susan had not been exactly tedious, but it had been very long, and for the last quarter of it Julia was troubled by her feet. In a way this was lucky, for in order to rest them she had voluntarily sat for ten solid minutes before a stained-glass window, thus surprising and pleasing her daughter very much indeed.

"We'll come again," promised Susan willingly. But neither surprise nor pleasure could blunt the edge of her critical intelligence; as they finally walked away she was busy with a rather damaging analogy between stained-glass windows and the poetry of James Elroy Flecker. They were both *easy;* and just as there were women at college who couldn't read Milton but adored *Hassan,* so her mother's eyes were evidently shut to a Gothic arch but open to a rose window. Susan was not so foolish, indeed, as to condemn either Flecker or stained glass out and out; she knew that both made excellent steppingstones, as it were, to better things; she only refused to countenance any confusion of the good with the best.

It was a neat analogy, and showed a great deal of intelligence; the only thing wrong with it was that it had nothing to do with the case. It was like Susan herself — strong on logic, weak on human nature. It left out Julia's feet.

So mother and daughter walked up the side of the promenade, Susan thinking in analogies, Julia thinking about her shoes, until they reached the long façade of the Pernollet Hotel. So many cars stood outside that Julia expressed her astonishment.

"They come from Aix," explained Susan. "People drive over for lunch. If Bryan hasn't got here early, we may have to wait for a table."

Bryan had been there half an hour, however, and was even then pressing Mrs. Packett to a second *apéritif*. Julia had one too; after so much architecture she felt she deserved it.

"We've ordered lunch," announced Bryan. "It ends with *fraises des bois*. You've just got here in time for them, Julia. Do you mind my calling you Julia — merely to prevent confusion?"

Julia looked across at the old lady. She herself would have preferred to be called Mrs. Packett — it helped to remind her of her new identity; but if the confusion idea originated with her mother-in-law, there was of course nothing to be said. Before the senior lady could speak, however, Susan had seized on the notion with warm approval. They would all call Julia, Julia; and Julia knew why. "It's to get out of calling me 'Mother,'" she thought, with a pang. Then philosophy and food came to her aid: it was very natural, — and she could never be really unhappy with a good lunch to eat and a restaurantful of people to look at. The clientele of the Pernollet, moreover, repaid attention; there were the local bourgeois, strong-stomached epicures intent on getting not only the best, but as much of it as possible, to whom a visit to Pernollet was something to be looked forward to for days and remembered for weeks; they sat for the most part in silence, eating steadily; and this silence, and the fact that they mostly wore black, and the amount they ate, somehow gave the impression that they were all celebrating substantial legacies. "Uncle Marius has done his duty; let us all — *Papa, Maman, Tante Mathilde, Monsieur le Notaire* — go and have a damned good lunch. . . ." As characteristic in their way, and a striking contrast, were the visitors from Aix — youths clad lightly and picturesquely *pour le sport,* gentlemen in English tweed, beautiful ladies looking like illustrations in *Vogue;* if they lacked the bourgeois solidity, they lacked also the bourgeois waistline; in their cars outside were the tennis-racquets and golf-clubs with which they held fat at bay. Their eating was carefree, the bourgeois's careless; and the shade of Brillat-Savarin must have been well content.

"Grand sight, isn't it?" murmured Bryan Relton.

Julia nodded. One of the visitors in particular was holding her attention — a young woman so exquisitely appointed, and so consciously superior, both to her host and to the Pernollet, that Julia had christened her the Disgusted Lady. She wore a huge white motor-coat, cut with the utmost elegance out of the coarsest linen, which — with an air of wishing to retain as many protective layers as possible between her person and her surroundings — she refused to take off. Julia was sorry for this, since she wanted to see what the Disgusted Lady wore underneath, but the gesture filled her with admiration. A string of pearls, a white buckskin sandal, were the only accessories visible: the Lady's head was bare, either because her fair Grecian curls were too beautiful to cover, or else, and more probably, because in the whole of France there wasn't a hat she would be seen dead in. Julia could just picture her at the milliner's, flinging model after model aside and sweeping disgustedly out. That such was her practice was evident from her companion's face, which wore a permanent expression of mingled pride and apology. He was a neat little man, about fifty, but he had no other character than that of being the Disgusted Lady's appendage.

"What a dreadful woman!" observed Susan, under her breath.

Julia looked round in surprise. She hadn't thought the Lady dreadful at all. A Terror, of course — but then a Terror of such magnificence!

"The one in the white coat," said Susan.

"It's a very nice coat," said Julia foolishly.

Bryan laughed.

"It was the very *best* butter," he said; and for some reason this idiotic remark made Susan laugh as well. Julia could see no joke whatever, but was only too glad to join in. In another moment she might have started to explain, and so made a fool of herself: for what she wanted to convey was at once so vague and so complicated as to be beyond her powers of expression. She felt, roughly speaking, that while the Disgusted Lady was probably a very disagreeable and useless person, she also made the world a more interesting place. She was a fascinating specimen of humanity, just as the mosquito is a fascinating specimen of dipterae. She repaid to the spectator the trouble she gave to her intimates. In short, she was worth having. "It takes all sorts to make a world," thought Julia.

But it was no use saying that to Susan.

## 4

Susan was a prig. Not an objectionable prig, not a proselytizing prig, but a prig from very excess of good qualities. Like all the right-minded young, she wanted perfection; the difficulty was that her standards of perfection were unusually high. Exquisite in her own integrity, she demanded an equal delicacy and up-rightness from her fellows. If they didn't come up to her standards, she would have no more to do with them. If she couldn't have the whole loaf, she would eat no bread at all. In Julia, who could extract nourish-ment from a crust, or even from a crumb, this attitude produced at first something like awe, then something like irritation. She found her daughter a paragon; she also, as has been said, found her a prig.

"She can't help it," thought Julia loyally, "she's been so beautifully brought up."

The latter part of this sentiment she expressed to Mrs. Packett, and the old lady was pleased.

"Everyone likes Susan," she said. "She was the most popular girl at school — they all wanted her to stay with them — and now it seems to be the same at college. She's always being put on committees."

Julia could well believe it. Susan was the committee-woman born — just, tactful, and graciously dignified. She ought to be an M.P.

"I used to be so glad," continued Mrs. Packett, her words chiming with Julia's thought, "that all the Suffragette business was over, so that if Susan ever went in for politics she could do it in a graceful and ladylike manner. We once heard her speak at a debate, and her grandfather said she had a positively masculine mind." Both Julia and Mrs. Packett were the kind of women pleased by such a remark. "If Bryan ever became Lord Chancellor, she'd make a splendid hostess for him."

Julia did not answer; not because she disagreed, but because in the first place she was very sure that Bryan would never become anything of the sort, and in the second because she was by this time a little tired of talking about other people. She wanted to talk about herself for a bit; but apart from the difficulty of finding a listener, she was not, in that company, a suitable topic.

"It must have been dreadful chaining oneself to the railings," said old Mrs. Packett suddenly; "but I'm sure I could have broken a shop-window."

5

The ease with which Julia settled down at Les Sapins was due possibly to the fact that she had arrived there tired out in both mind and body; she was quite content, for the moment, to sit quietly in the sun, and go for short walks about the garden, and eat appetizing meals at regular intervals. She read the *Continental Daily Mail* and darned her stockings. She took a nap every afternoon. From Mrs. Packett she learnt several games of patience, and she also found, in a cupboardful of old books, an English manual of fortunetelling. Julia adored telling fortunes, and treated herself to three a day; the best of the three was the one she believed. This occupation brought her into friendly relations with Anthelmine the cook, who used to come up behind, as Julia sat dealing her cards at a garden table, and utter loud exclamations of sympathy and surprise. She exclaimed particularly over the three of spades, which in Julia's system stood for no more than a Slight Disappointment; but since Anthelmine, unlike Claudia, spoke no English, Julia never discovered why. She thought of asking Susan to find out, but dreaded her daughter's disapproval. Anthelmine only looked on, of course, but she now and then sat down to do so; she had an imposing figure — not tall, indeed, but so broad in the beam that three cats at once could take their ease in her shadow — and she was naturally hard on her feet. Julia herself did not mind Anthelmine's sitting down, but she sometimes feared that to Susan, passing afar in the vine, it might seem that her mother was playing cards with the cook. . . .

"And I would, too," Julia accused herself sorrowfully. "I've got no dignity." But she did not drive Anthelmine away, and Anthelmine, who was too valuable in a kitchen to fear anybody, asked Susan point-blank whether Madame her mother would like a pistachio cream. Julia was not particularly pleased by this compliment — she felt it too definitely underlined her proclivity for low company — but she finished a second helping of the cream, and but for Bryan, who ate faster, would have finished a third as well. "Done you there!" said the look in Bryan's eye; but Julia ignored it. Ignoring that young man's eye, indeed, had already become second nature to her; she feared its bright intelligence, its perpetual questioning. Contrary to her daughter's express desire, she was making no attempt whatever to get to know him; she was too much afraid that *he* might get to know *her*. Her function at Les Sapins was that of a *dea ex machina;* and the make of her car would not bear examining.

"I can lie low for another day or two," thought Julia, uneasily aware that she was neglecting her duties. But she did not really worry. Worrying was never natural to her; in that clear, fresh, pine-scented air — with all those regular, delicious, abundant meals — it was a physical impossibility. And though Susan and Bryan were evidently very fond of each other, Julia had no fear of their mutual passion flaming into any reckless and irretrievable blaze.

"There's no hurry," thought Julia comfortably. Her spirit was like a plump cat on a sunny wall. It purred. But there was a boy underneath getting ready to chase her off.

### 6

"What shall you do this afternoon?" asked Susan after lunch on the fourth day.

Julia, who had her answer ready, gave it with some complacence.

"I'm going on the terrace to read *The Forsyte Saga.*" She was glad Susan had asked; it wasn't boastfulness, she just wanted her daughter to know. But Susan's smile — how extraordinary! — was less respectful than indulgent.

"Grandmother adores it," she said. "You'll have a lovely peaceful afternoon."

Thus affectionately put in her place among the senile, Julia went out on the terrace in an extremely unliterary frame of mind; and this in a way was fortunate, since the afternoon, though lovely, was not destined to be peaceful. Scarcely had she settled herself when her potential son-in-law appeared with purposeful looks and an avowed desire for conversation.

"Go and talk to Sue," directed Julia. "I'm reading."

He glanced at her book — again, how odd! — with exactly the same expression as Susan's; then shut it without a word and flung himself down where he could look directly into her face. In spite of her annoyance at such cavalier manners, Julia could not help admitting that he was extremely attractive.

"Look here," he said abruptly, "what have you got against me?"

The attack was so sudden that Julia for once lacked presence of mind. Instead of protesting, she merely stared. Bryan hurried on.

"Because you have, darling, and it's no use saying you haven't. I can feel it. If you were anyone else I should say you were still sore over that rise I got out of you the first morning."

"Rubbish!" cried Julia indignantly.

"As you say. And what's all the more puzzling to me is that right from the beginning — right from *then* — I thought we were going to get on. As soon as I saw you, I thought, 'Good!' If you were a bit disapproving at lunch, I'd deserved it and didn't mind. But you've been disapproving ever since, and it isn't natural."

"Got a good conceit of yourself, haven't you?" said Julia.

He looked quite hurt.

"I never thought we should have to have all this beating about the bush, either. I should have thought that if you disliked my ties or my table manners you'd tell me straight out, and probably box my ears into the bargain. I expected any number of black eyes, Julia darling, but not the frozen mitt."

The statement was so outrageous that Julia, who had been behaving like a perfect lady for four solid days, could not let it pass.

"Do I *look* the sort of person who gives black eyes?" she demanded.

"Yes, you do, darling. You are. Just as I'm the sort of person who gets them. The fact of the matter is — "

Julia beat the bush no longer, but finished for him.

"You're the same kind as I am," she said grimly.

It was out, and she felt a certain relief; but she was also resentful. He had chased her off the sunny wall of her self-complacency; he had shown that her impersonation of a lady was not so good as she had thought. Worse still, he was going to make her say things, do things, that would have a definite effect; that might lead to scenes with Susan, to explanations with Mrs. Packett; that would put an end, in short, to the happy period of her carefree basking. . . .

"Well," said Bryan, looking at her under his lids, "that's not such a bad sort to be — is it?"

— 111 —

Julia did not immediately reply. To marshal her thoughts, to produce an ordered sequence of ideas, was not a business which came easily to her. She had first to disentangle her own meaning, then to fit it with words; and since what she now had to communicate was of the utmost importance, so the preliminaries were correspondingly long.

"Not *bad*," she said at last. "Not out-and-out *bad*. But bad compared with people like Susan and her grandmother. Compared with other people, we're quite good. If you ask me," said Julia, "we're sort of half-and-halves. So long as we stay with our own lot, we're all right. We don't do any harm. It's only when we begin to mix with the others — with the real good — that trouble starts. If you married Susan, you'd make her miserable."

"You married Susan's father," said Bryan swiftly.

Julia shrugged.

"That was different. It was the war. If he hadn't been killed, I should have made *him* miserable."

"You'd have given him a damned good time."

"It's not a good time they want," said Julia soberly. "They want a different sort of time altogether. I'm rotten at explaining. But I remember when Susan was coming, and after, how good they were to me — you see, you can't say a thing about them without bringing in *good* — and yet we couldn't get on. They really wanted me, too; they wanted to have me for a daughter, and I was so grateful, especially as I'd half-expected to be thrown out on my neck; I thought I could do anything in the world for them. *I* tried, and *they* tried; but it didn't work."

The young man moved impatiently. "It's all dead and gone to him," thought Julia.

"I admit all that," he said; "but you must see it's a very different thing, my marrying Susan. We're both young, we're in love with each other — "

"What are you going to *do* with yourself?" interrupted Julia. "You're a sort of lawyer, aren't you?"

"A barrister, darling. At any rate, I've been called. But I'm not sure I shall ever practise."

"Why not?"

"Too much of a grind. I don't want to spend the next ten years grinding. I want to knock about the world and look at things and talk to people. I got five hundred a year from my mother, and if I married Susan I dare say the old man would stump up a bit more. He'll adore her."

Julia's thoughts flew back to the dressing-room at the Frivolity, and to the recumbent figure of Sir James Relton. Bryan was quite right: to a daughter-in-law like Susan the old rip would be generous indeed. He'd know what he was getting. And then Susan would no doubt have money too; together she and Bryan

would be able to knock about — first-class — to their
hearts' content. Only — would Susan's heart thus be
contented? Did she realize what lay in store for her?
"I don't believe they know a thing about each other,"
thought Julia. . . .

"I see your idea," continued Bryan tolerantly; "but
— if you'll excuse my saying so — it's all wrong."

"If I had my way," said Julia, following her own
train of thought, "I'd pack you off for a month together and let you find out for yourselves."

Bryan grinned.

"There's nothing I'd like better, darling."

"I've no doubt there isn't," said Julia sharply. "Why
don't you suggest it to her?"

"Because — "

"Because you know she'd send you packing in double-
quick time."

"Not at all," corrected Bryan, with a sudden return
to dignity. "Because, as I should have thought you'd
know, a fellow feels very differently about a girl he's
going to marry and a girl he just wants to . . . have
fun with. He feels — well, scrupulous."

Julia looked at him.

"You ought to have seen your face just now," she
said. "There wasn't a scruple in sight."

The last word, this time, was hers.

## 7

She did not, however, get much pleasure from it. She was ruffled, put out, and more than ever convinced that she would soon have to make herself extremely unpopular. And popularity, to Julia, was the breath of life: she would rather shine at a coffee-stall than eat a good dinner unnoticed. "They'll never understand," thought Julia dismally. "They'll just think I want to throw my weight about." She sighed deeply. There was another thing — her weight! She was almost certain that her stays felt tighter than they did a week ago. They weren't the sort that laced, either: they had a good stout zip-fastener, full strength. . . .

It was thus in no cheerful frame of mind that Julia ascended the stone steps and met her hostess at the top. Mrs. Packett, however, looked pleased; she held a letter in her hand, and was evidently full of news.

"Sir William comes next week!" she said. "He's Susan's guardian, you know, and so charming!"

"A man!" thought Julia.

The black clouds of depression still enveloped her; but she perceived a slight rift.

# Chapter 10

Every morning, just as Julia herself had done in that long-ago time at Barton, Susan arranged the flowers. But with her it was a labour of love; she picked not only the roses, but wild flowers as well, making what she called "tangles" of them — large, and to Julia's eye rather straggling, bouquets that died almost the next day. Susan didn't seem to mind: every morning she went up into the vine and picked more. Some of them were really pretty, thin sprays of forget-me-not with tiny flowers, and clover with big purple heads, and something tall and tough that had bright blue rosettes growing all down the stem. But Susan didn't stop even there. She actually picked grass, and dead bits of twig.

"I believe you like the tangles best," said Julia once, in her astonishment.

"Yes," agreed Susan. They were in the old garden-room, next door to the kitchen, where Susan kept her vases amongst the cobwebs and firewood. Bryan lounged in the doorway, idle as Julia: they had both expressed a wish to be of use, but so halfheartedly that even Susan's good manners had permitted her to refuse.

"Why?" asked Julia.

"Because I can do so much more with them."

Julia looked at a mass of yellow roses triumphant in their cream jar.

"They don't make half so much show as *those* . . . ?"

"No," admitted Susan. "But *that* — that's just the roses themselves. I've done hardly anything. A tangle makes a show because of *me*."

Involuntarily Julia glanced towards the door; but if this explanation reached Bryan's ears, he gave no sign. Or perhaps he didn't realize how complete an explanation it was, or how particularly ominous to a young man who didn't want to do anything special, but just knock around the world. Their conversation of the previous day was still fresh in Julia's mind; but there was something else on her mind as well, and she did not, as she no doubt should have done, seize the opportunity of showing Bryan up.

Instead, she said casually, "Aren't we expecting another visitor? Your grandmother said something — ?"

Susan looked up from her flowers.

"That's Uncle William. He isn't an uncle really, of course, but I've always called him that. He's a dear. He's coming the day after to-morrow."

"To inspect me," observed Bryan from the doorway. Julia ignored the interruption.

"Sir William, isn't he?" she asked.

"Sir William Waring. He was a great friend of Grandfather's."

That made him seventy at least, thought Julia gloomily. Men of seventy had no interest for her: they were always, in her experience, either doddering or spry; and the spry were the worst.

"About fifty-one," said Bryan, who had been watching her face.

Julia ignored him again.

"And have you," she asked Susan cunningly, "an Auntie as well?"

"Unmarried," said Bryan.

Susan glanced at him sharply. "Are you meaning," said that look — and a very Packett look it was — "to make fun of my mother? I do not suspect you," said that look, "of deliberate impertinence; but aren't you a little forgetting yourself?"

Warm gratitude flooded Julia's breast; it was sweet to be so protected by one's daughter, and for a moment that sweetness was all she felt. Then under her pleasure, marring it, stirred a feeling of guilt, almost of shame. For she didn't deserve such protection: Susan was wrong, and Bryan right. Bryan, because his own thoughts no doubt worked the same way, knew what she, Julia, was getting at: Susan's lovely mind never even suspected it. Yet from all this complication of wrongs and rights emerged one certain good: Susan had, possibly for the first time, recognized and admitted in her lover something alien to herself.

"She's never seen him against his own background," thought Julia. "It's queer that I should be it." She looked at her daughter's stern face, and at once Susan smiled. It was the most loving smile Julia had ever received from her. "Let her find *him* out without finding me out too," prayed Julia selfishly; "I shan't be here long, O Lord!"

"Lady Waring," said Susan, addressing herself pointedly to her mother, "died about ten years ago. I hardly remember her, except that she was very nice. They never had any children: I expect that was why they made such a fuss of me."

"It must be dreadful to have no children, with a title," said Julia seriously. "It seems such waste."

Susan laughed. Like a good schoolmistress, she knew that severity should be tempered with kindness, and having properly frozen the atmosphere, she now proceeded to thaw it again.

"Uncle William isn't a baronet — he's a mere knight. He was something in the Admiralty, and they knighted him after the war. Will you have roses for your room, or a tangle?"

"A tangle," said Julia. She still liked the roses best, but she wanted to show her gratitude.

Bryan lounged in and swung himself onto the table. "What about me?" he asked. "What about my room?"

"You've flowers enough," said Susan. "You've still the whole bunch we picked yesterday."

"But I want one now, from you. Give me a rose, Susan."

Flushed, smiling, very pretty, she broke off a yellow bud. Bryan received it with suitable gratitude. But his eyes were not on Susan; they looked over her shoulder, at Julia, with defiance.

2

That afternoon, immediately after lunch, Julia set out to look at a tree. Both Susan and Mrs. Packett were able to contemplate trees for minutes together, and her natural spirit of emulation made Julia covet the same power. There must, she thought, be something in it: some esoteric connection between garden-seats and the gentility she so much admired. For her daughter and mother-in-law were by no means isolated examples: every real lady Julia had ever met — most of whom, indeed, she had encountered actually at Barton — showed the same idiosyncrasy. On the

Tuesday afternoon, therefore, Julia went out to have a whack at it herself.

She had selected her object the day before — a small *mirabelle* plum covered with hard yellowish fruit. Compared with the pines, to be sure, it had something of a twopence-coloured look; but for that very reason Julia felt it would be easier. She could work up to pines later on.

The *mirabelle* was situated on the second terrace, and as she walked up the zigzag path, dragging a garden-chair, Julia conscientiously looked about her. It was very pretty, and all the prettier because the vines were badly neglected. Between their rows the ground was green and sweet with clover and wild strawberry: where the wires had broken, full-leaved garlands, tinted turquoise-blue by sulphate, drooped and mingled with the tall flowering grass. All this Julia saw, and to a certain extent enjoyed; but the chair had a knack of hitting against her ankles, and she determined to put off all serious appreciation until she was comfortably seated. The path wound up: at the second angle it passed through a little grove of nut trees, some springing from the edge of the vine, some from the side of a great outcropping rock. There were steps cut in its base, and by peering through the nut boughs Julia could see the dilapidated shell of a tiny pavilion. But she did not allow it to distract her; she mounted steadily on, growing hotter and hotter, to the second terrace and the *mirabelle* plum.

"I'm going to bake," thought Julia, as she set up her chair; and indeed the whole circle of the plain, on whose circumference she was placed, shimmered under a heat mist. In it the roofs and steeples of Belley, the smaller groupings of the villages, showed bright yet insubstantial; here and there, exquisitely distributed over the flat, rose small cone-shaped hills, each neatly girdled by a ring of poplars, and belonging, in that light, less to Agriculture than to Art. It was the landscape of a holy picture, in which saints, not peasants, should have enlivened the foreground; and Julia needed no more than one glance to identify it as a lovely view.

She then settled back in her chair, looked at the time, and gave her eyes and mind to the plum tree. It leaned gracefully towards her, as though sensible of the compliment; its small hard fruit, already faintly speckled, made her think of bird's eggs. They would look pretty in a mossy basket — like plovers'; and Julia wondered when they would be ripe. Would the nuts have been ripe, that she passed in the little thicket? From above they looked no more than bushes, the rock was a mere boulder, the pavilion a toy. Its roof peaked up like the roof of a pagoda: a stray architect, long before the Packetts came, had identified it as late eighteenth-century chinoiserie. But Julia's interest was purely human; what a place, she thought, for assignations! Did Susan ever meet Bryan there, when the house slept and a moon shone through the nut trees? But the bushes about the steps grew thick and undisturbed; Julia very much feared that the pavilion was being wasted. Poor thing, it would probably be quite glad of someone — glad to hear a kiss again, to be filled with delicious stifled laughter and the murmuring of lover's vows. . . .

"I bet it's seen a thing or two in its time," thought Julia.

She looked at her watch. She had been sitting there twelve and a half minutes — practically a quarter of an hour. To stay longer, in that heat, would be little short of dangerous, so she folded her chair again and went down into the cool.

She was feeling extremely pleased with herself; but pride, notoriously, goes before a fall.

### 3

Returning by the front door, she found Susan, Bryan and the postman all in a group on the steps.

"*Il y a quelqu'erreur*," Susan was saying firmly. "Bryan, give it back at once."

Always ready to join anything that looked like a crowd, Julia paused and craned over his shoulder. The object which Susan so eagerly repudiated was a picture postcard of extreme vulgarity.

"What things they do think of!" began Julia, much interested; and the next moment felt Bryan's elbow hard against her ribs. Susan was standing with a stony and averted face.

Furious with herself, still more furious with Bryan for the very reason that she should have been grateful to him, Julia drew back.

"Perhaps there isn't a mistake after all," said Susan.

Bryan turned the card over so that Julia could see. It was addressed to "Mrs. Packard," and in the space for correspondence was scrawled a tender message from Fred Genocchio.

In spite of herself Julia felt the blood rise till she stood blushing like a schoolgirl. Ardently, violently, did she long to deny all knowledge of the thing; yet she had at the same time an obscure feeling that to do so would be to deny Fred himself. As though he had appeared on those steps in person, and she had cut him. . . .

So torn, she could not find a word to say; and at last Susan spoke for her.

"*C'est bien,*" she said calmly, addressing the postman. "*J'ai mal lu.* Coming up the vine, Bryan?"

What with anger, mortification, and sentiment —
the emotions called forth, in that order, by Bryan,
Susan, and Mr. Genocchio, — Julia was glad to be left
alone. The card now lay, in theory still unclaimed,
on the stone balustrade; she took it up and bore it to
her room. Fred had not written much, only four words;
but a whole sonnet sequence could hardly have affected
her more. *"Still thinking about you, Fred."* He was
still thinking about her! Despite her incredible hard-
heartedness, amid the excitement and bustle of his professional affairs, he still thought of her! In her gratitude
for the sentiment conveyed Julia almost forgave the tact-
lessness of the vehicle. For after all, it wasn't so bad.
It wasn't *dirty*. He probably just chose it to try and
cheer her up a bit, in case she was feeling blue. . . .

"Then he shouldn't have," thought Julia, veering
round again. "What business has he to think I'm not
being happy? Conceit, that's what it is. Sheer conceit.
He probably thinks I'm crying my eyes out for
him!"

Then she sat down and cried hard.


4

From her seat under the pine trees old Mrs. Packett
watched Susan and Bryan going up through the vine.
Susan was a little ahead, walking as usual as though

all gradients were alike to her; Bryan, his hands in his pockets, loped easily behind, taking long strides over the rough places, lagging on the smooth. They made a charming pair, thought Mrs. Packett: she had just said so, in the letter she was writing to Sir William.

My daughter-in-law [continued old Mrs. Packett] seems to like him too; but she is very properly reserving her opinion, and I think she agrees with me that Susan is too young. It has all turned out *perfectly smoothly;* as you know, I was *apprehensive* (about Julia coming here), but I am glad to say that I was wrong. I feel sure that you and she between you will be able to make Susan see reason. I want you to get on with her, William, and knowing your prejudices I am going to warn you now not to be put off by her appearance, which is a little *florid*. But she is really most pleasant and amiable, quite contented in this very quiet place, and I have a feeling that everything will turn out well. When I look ahead a few years D.V. and see Susan married, and perhaps great-grandchildren, and Julia with her nice little cake-shop, which I shall run up to town to inspect, I feel myself to be a very lucky old woman.

Such was Mrs. Packett's view of the situation; and by a curious coincidence the amiable Julia, having wiped her eyes and blown her nose, was even then presenting the very same view to a very different recipient.

## 5

She wrote: —

Dear Fred, —

Thank you for your card, though I won't say it wasn't a bit common, but I know you meant well. This is a lovely place, large house and gardens and a private vineyard with most lovely views. My daughter is the loveliest girl you ever saw, so fair and distinguished, and a real daughter to me. I am having a thorough rest and holiday, and enjoying it very much. How is Ma? Poor old bird, she wasn't half done up, was she. I often think of you all, and hope you are all having every success and the hand you all deserve.

Yours sincerely, —

JULIA PACKETT.

Don't send me any more of those postcards, Fred; the servants here are French, and you know what their dirty minds are.

Yours, —

JULIA.

When it was finished she looked at his card and addressed an envelope to the Casino Bleu and to the house at Maida Vale. She had no French stamps, but there were some in the billiard-room; Susan and Mrs. Packett kept books of them, in the writing-table drawer.

Julia stepped out into the corridor and there paused. Could she just *take* a stamp, or ought she to pay for it? A lady, undoubtedly (thought Julia) would leave the money. She went back and fetched her bag; and on opening it in the billiard-room made the alarming discovery that when she had sent her letter to Fred Genocchio she would have only five francs left.

For almost the first time in her life Julia's courage failed. To be penniless in London was nothing; even in Paris — full of English and Americans as it was — she would not have despaired; but to be penniless among the Packetts! It was a blow so great that her knees absolutely gave under it. She sat down on the nearest chair, her bag still open on her lap, and contemplated the disaster with terrified eyes.

She ought to have thought, of course. She ought to have realized. But she had been so taken up with simply getting there, so unused to looking more than a week ahead that — well, that she just hadn't. And even if she had, from whom could she have borrowed? Who — more to the point — could she borrow from now? Involuntarily, Julia shook her head: if the sources had been dry when she left London, it would take more than long-distance work to make them flow afresh. Personality, that was what did it; and you couldn't, at least Julia couldn't, put personality into a letter. She had to be *there*. If she were only there now, she felt, she could borrow blood from a stone.

She could borrow from anyone in the world except Mrs. Packett, and Susan, and Bryan Relton.

Only the world, to all intents and purposes, had at the moment no other inhabitants.

After tracing this vicious circle for perhaps the twentieth time, Julia also remembered that she had no return ticket.

## 6

Up in the vine Bryan was trying to make Susan quarrel with him. The occasion was purely artificial — a disagreement over the title of a book — but her cool serenity, her perfect control, was a perpetual challenge to him. He wanted to break it down, to see her hot and ruffled; it was the deep impulse to mastery which she would never satisfy. Julia, when she saw Bryan as a pursuer, was right; but she was thinking in physical terms only: if the material pursuit had been all — if by following Susan half across France he could finally have captured her — his attachment would already have worn thin. For a day or two, indeed, the apparent ease of his victory had actually disconcerted and disappointed him; he felt like a man who, setting out to climb some just-accessible peak, finds a funicular railway already installed. The railway, fortunately, did not work; though Susan had accepted him within a week of his arrival at the villa, what now bound him to her was the knowledge that he had never made any real impression on her at all.

"Why can't you admit you may be mistaken?" asked Susan patiently.

"Why can't you?"

"Perhaps I am," said Susan at once. "Anyway, it's on Grandmother's dressing-table, and I'll look when we go in."

So that quarrel came to nothing. Susan would look, as she promised, and if Bryan was right she would come and tell him at once, and if he was wrong she would wait until he asked. She was perfect, both in justice and in magnanimity.

"The lavender's nearly out," said Susan, to change the subject.

They were sitting on a high gravelly slope which some bygone owner of the villa had laid out with long flower-borders; but only lavender now survived, flourishing in a bushy grey-green hedge that was sweetened but not yet coloured by the thick flower-spikes. Susan reached up and broke off a twig.

"Smell," she said, rubbing it against Bryan's nose.

He seized her hand and, still holding it, rolled over and buried his face in her palm. The smell of the lavender, the smell of Susan's warm sun-browned skin, made the blood in his temples drum.

"Susan," he said, "darling, I'm not going to wait three years."

"You won't have to," said Susan steadily.

"But if they don't budge?"

"As soon as I'm twenty-one."

"Even that's another eight months."

"Can't you wait eight months?"

For a long minute Bryan lay still. He was thinking of something Julia had said, and wondering how much of Julia was alive in her daughter. None, Julia had implied; but was she right? What did parents ever really know of their children? Bryan's thoughts flew to his finances: he had still a traveller's cheque for fifty pounds — enough to take Susan to Como, or to Rome, or perhaps down to the Riviera. . . .

He turned over and sat up. That was his mistake.

"Susan —" he said.

He stopped. He oughtn't to have looked at her. With his face still buried in her palm he might have spoken; but not under that clear level gaze.

"Well?" said she.

"Nothing. It's teatime. Let's go down."

Hand in hand they descended the path. In the nut grove they kissed. But they were not contented.

# Chapter 11

For some five minutes Julia and Mrs. Packett had the tea-table to themselves. Both were preoccupied, Julia with the devastating problem of her finances, Mrs. Packett, as will be seen, less unhappily.

"I've been making a list," she announced, "of people in town who would like your cakes. I've got fifteen names already."

"I wish you wouldn't trouble," said Julia sincerely.

"It's no trouble, my dear, it's a pleasure. You must get out a nice card, and I'll enclose it with my letter. I believe Kensington would be a good place, because Susan tells me it's full of flats."

Julia looked up in surprise.

"I've never noticed it," she said. "I think they're as sharp in Kensington as anywhere else."

"They haven't proper kitchens," explained Mrs. Packett, not quite taking her daughter-in-law's point. "Just a sort of cupboard and a sink, and you can't make cakes in a place like that. I'm sure you'll do well. Where *is* Susan?"

"Coming down the path," said Julia.

The young people, indeed, were close upon them, having run the last few yards in an ebullition of good spirits very pleasant to see. "Dear children!" murmured Mrs. Packett. "Damn!" said Julia softly. She wasn't damning anyone in particular, least of all Susan; she was just railing at that fate which had planted her down penniless in the one place where being penniless mattered.

"The view's wonderful to-day," said Susan. "You ought to go up."

"I went up after lunch," said Julia. Susan was evidently trying to show that the incident of the postcard had now been forgiven, and Julia in turn exerted herself to appear bright and affable. She praised the view very highly, and described in some detail the appearance of the *mirabelle* plum. In other circumstances it was just the sort of conversation she would have enjoyed, but for once the spectacle of her own beautiful behaviour gave Julia no pleasure. She relapsed into silence, and let the others talk on.

It was very hot. Their table under the pines was in deep shadow, but even through those serried branches the sun here and there managed to penetrate. There was a disc of gold in Mrs. Packett's lap, another on

Susan's hair; the ground from Bryan's chair to Julia's was hatched with light and shadow. Presently they were all silent together, and in the pause, from high overhead, came a staccato tap like the tapping of a knuckle on a door.

"There's a woodpecker," said Susan softly.

They all listened; the obliging bird at once tapped again. "It might be a call-boy," thought Julia. Ah, if only it were! If she were only back in a dressing-room somewhere — perhaps with bananas on her head — what would it matter that she hadn't a penny in her pocket? There would be other girls to borrow from, and boys in front, and maybe one particular boy waiting to take her out to supper! "I'd eat fried fish and be grateful," thought Julia, from the heart. Nostalgia overwhelmed her: she wanted to be back among her own kind, among people who expected you to be broke, who took it as the natural thing, who were mostly broke themselves and so could understand. "Fried fish!" thought Julia passionately. "I'd eat winkles on a pin . . ."

"One of these days," Bryan was saying, "we ought to go over to Aix."

Susan raised her eyebrows.

"What for?"

"Oh, just for the ride. To amuse Julia."

The sound of her own name brought Julia back

to the present. But even the thought of an excursion could not cheer her. It would only mean spending money. . . .

"I'm very well here," she said. "I like the quiet."

"Anyway, you'd hate Aix," Susan assured her. "It's full of visitors rushing about in cars. All those casino towns are the same."

Julia sat up. A casino — and a casino within reach! Hope, never long absent from her, fluttered back into her breast — no modest olive-bearing dove, but a peacock spreading its gorgeous tail. With five francs, at a casino, you could make a fortune! You could break the bank and come home a millionaire! Julia knew nothing about gambling save that beginners always won, and that it was a good plan (if you weren't a beginner and so lost) to pretend to shoot yourself, and wait till the croupiers had stuffed your pockets with cash, and then get up and walk off. Either way was money for jam, and Julia was so starved for excitement that she almost hoped the second course would be necessary. But she wouldn't shoot herself: she would pretend to take poison — an aspirin would do — and drop down in a graceful appealing pose. She could see herself doing it. And perhaps the man who found her would be not a croupier but an American millionaire, and in that case she would let him bring her back to life, and he would fall in love with her and drive her about in a car the size of a house and a motor-coat like the Disgusted Lady's. If he were the right kind of American — no, an English peer would be better — she might even marry him, and so give Susan a titled stepfather.

So Julia's peacock spread its magnificent tail, and Julia, lost in contemplation of it, had been some minutes alone with her daughter before she realized that both Bryan and Mrs. Packett had taken themselves off.

"Have you talked to Grandmother yet?" asked Susan abruptly.

## 2

"About Bryan? Yes, of course I have." In spite of herself Julia could not quite repress a sigh. She didn't want to talk about Bryan, she wanted to go on with her beautiful dreams, to visualize more distinctly the English peer, to rehearse scraps of her conversation with him. What was Bryan to her, beside that noble and fascinating figure? However, she knew her duty; and in any case, Susan would not have let her escape it.

"Of course I have," said Julia again.

"And can you do anything? Is she beginning to see how — how silly it is?" asked Susan eagerly.

Julia hesitated. Here was an opportunity, if she wanted one, to clear up the whole situation — to disclaim the rôle of ally and range herself definitely on the other side; but by doing so she would lose whatever influence she possessed. At present she was free, so to speak, of both camps; and so uncomfortably situated, with one foot in each, she feared she should remain a little longer.

"It isn't silly at all," Julia said (speaking from the Packett camp). "At any rate" (she changed over) "from her point of view. You *are* very young, Susan, and you haven't finished at college — "

"I could take my degree after I was married," said Susan quickly.

Julia thought this a very odd idea indeed. But it gave her hope.

"Only it wouldn't be the same, would it? You couldn't live in — "

"In residence," prompted Susan.

" — in residence, then, and have all the fun you do now? *Why* can't you wait, Sue?"

"I don't want to," said Susan obstinately.

It was her only argument; on it her beautiful mouth closed in a stubborn line.

"If you're thinking of Bryan — " began Julia again.

"Of course I'm thinking of Bryan. No one else does.

No one else seems to realize that they're asking him to wait three years too."

"Oh, well," said Julia easily, "I expect he'd manage."

All at once, for one moment, Susan's composure cracked.

"I've no doubt he would," she said tartly; and with the colour high in her cheeks got up and walked away.

Julia sat on alone. "So that's it!" she was thinking. "So *that*'s it!"


### 3

She was very sorry for Susan. She was sorry for any young girl who discovers that her lover is not perfect in fidelity; and though in this case it was undoubtedly a good thing that Susan should begin to see Bryan as he was, Julia at that moment felt more sympathetic to her than ever before. She was sympathetic, she was sorry; but she neither sympathized nor sorrowed long. Susan and her troubles could wait: the immediate problem was how she, Julia, was going to get to Aix.

Her five francs, the foundation of her prospective fortune, must be preserved intact; and for some moments Julia toyed with the idea of revising her attitude to a family excursion. If they all went together Mrs. Packett would pay for a car, and the question of transport would thus be solved; on the other hand, such a plan would considerably hamper her own freedom of movement. She might not be able to reach the casino alone, and Julia had no intention of poisoning herself in the presence of her daughter. Susan would simply produce an emetic.

"I've got to get there by myself," thought Julia, "and I've got to get there free . . ."

For perhaps half an hour she sat pondering, while the garden cooled and the hillside began to glow. A great dragonfly swooped among the rosebushes: in the perfect stillness the creak of returning oxwains, on the Magnieu road, was distinctly audible. But Julia's thoughts were exclusively urban; she had returned in spirit to the shifts and manœuvres of her London life. The present terrain was unfamiliar to her; she could see no further than Belley; she did not even know in which direction her Tom Tiddler's ground lay. . . .

But it has been mentioned before that Julia was very resourceful, and by the time the last of the sun had faded from the vine her plans were cut and dried. She had remembered, in a beautiful heart-lifting flash, the string of cars outside the Pernollet

Hotel. They came, Susan had told her, from Aix; to Aix they would doubtless return; and if she couldn't get a lift from a well-fed Frenchman — well, she wasn't the good old Julia she used to be.

# Chapter 12

At twelve o'clock the following morning Julia began to listen for the lunch-bell. Its punctual sounding was of great importance to her: if the meal was over, as it usually was, by half-past one, she would have an hour and a half for the four-mile walk into Belley, since the patrons of the Pernollet would hardly get away before three. Coffee was the danger-point. On dull days they took it in the dining-room, and never sat more than ten minutes; but if the day were fine they adjourned to the garden, where Mrs. Packett at least had a tendency to linger. And the day was fine, blue and golden, with a light breeze. Julia was glad in a way, since it enabled her to wear her white linen suit (to which, before she left, she planned to add a large yellow taffeta bow); but she couldn't help fidgeting. Mrs. Packet, instead of coming straight out, went to her room; they had to wait for her; and when she did come Susan, always particular, sent the milk back to be heated afresh.

"I'll take mine black," said Julia.

She gulped it down and put the cup back on the table. Susan had a book with her, Bryan looked half-asleep; in two minutes Mrs. Packett would be asleep as well. Julia pushed back her chair and prepared for flight.

"Do you know how to make shortbread?" asked Mrs. Packett, opening her eyes.

"Yes," said Julia recklessly. "I believe I'll go for a walk."

But Mrs. Packett, like so many of the old, heard only what interested her.

"Which sort of butter do you use — salt or fresh?"

"Fresh," said Julia.

"I always use salt," said Mrs. Packett. "I must make you some. And I'll show you my special maids-of-honour."

"That will be lovely," said Julia.

"And almond buns. I always think — "

"Lovely," said Julia again. "I shall enjoy it like anything. I know how clever you are. I believe I'll go for a good walk."

It was the reappearance of Anthelmine that saved her. For Anthelmine brought out not only the milk, but also a fine plump chicken offered for sale by the man who looked after the vine; and Mrs. Packett, an expert in poultry, naturally forgot everything else while she poked it in the chest. She poked, weighed, and finally approved; and when she turned back to the coffee table, her daughter-in-law was gone.

The road to Belley covered nearly four miles, and the day was hot; but Julia — a yellow bow round her neck, her hat over one eye — did not care a damn. She felt extraordinarily lighthearted. She had a smile for everyone she met, and nearly caused the death of two bicycling *poilus* who kept turning round to wave to her. Julia waved back. She waved also to the car which had so narrowly missed them. Soon, very softly, she was singing as she walked.

She sang the Marseillaise.

She had reverted to type.

## 2

Her first act on reaching Belley was to sit down under a tree on the promenade and overhaul her face. It didn't look bad, considering the long walk, and with the help of lipstick and rouge and a touch of eyebrow-pencil she was soon as fresh as a daisy. No mere daisy, however, could display such handsome tints as those in which Julia now blossomed forth; she was not actu. ally painted, but she was perceptibly made-up. When she had quite finished she walked once past the big café by the bus stop (just to make sure she had got

the effects right) and then turned up the other side
of the promenade towards the Pernollet Hotel.

There were four cars standing outside, but only
one with a G.B. plate. Julia strolled by and looked at
it carefully: it was an old but well-kept Daimler, in
charge of an elderly but spruce chauffeur; on the
back seat lay a couple of air-cushions, a couple of
English magazines, and a large plaid rug. The French
cars, standing behind, were all two-seaters, of the
sort which gentlemen do not usually drive alone; and
after some consideration Julia decided to stick to her
own nationality. She looked at the Daimler once more,
noted that the magazines were the *Strand* and the
*Cornhill;* then walked a little way down the street
and, with a philosophic sigh, wiped off most of her
lipstick.

As she turned back she saw that she had been right:
the owners of the car, who were just getting in,
matched it perfectly. They were two middle-aged
Englishwomen of the type so ably caricatured in the
French press; their resemblance to horses was not
strict, but it was there. As the second flat back disappeared Julia moved forward and put her head in
after it.

"Excuse me," she said quietly — in her best Packett
manner — "but are you by any chance going back to
Aix?"

The Misses Marlowe, after recovering from their surprise, quite pleasantly admitted that they were.

"Then I wonder," continued Julia, "whether I might possibly ask you for a lift? I find there isn't a bus till four, and my children will be waiting for me."

The ladies consulted each other by a glance. If Julia had moved away they could have consulted verbally, and the younger, who had just read a novel by A. E. W. Mason, might have developed scruples; but Julia did not budge. She stayed where she was, half in the car already, and in consequence was not refused.

"Of course," said the elder lady, "certainly"; and Julia nipped in.

It was a pleasant journey. The car moved swiftly and easily along, and the two Samaritans had no cause to regret their kindness. For their new companion proved most interesting, and told them many amusing anecdotes about the three children — Ronald, Rachel and Elizabeth — whom she had left with their governess at Aix.

"I say *left*," smiled Julia, with pleasant humour, "but I've only been away from them three hours. I fancied Miss Graham — my governess — wanted them to herself for a while. I believe she thinks I'm bad for discipline."

"After all, they're on holiday," said Miss Marlowe indulgently.

Julia nodded.

"That's what I say. And they do lessons every morning. French, you know. That's why I brought them here."

"You don't find Aix too relaxing?" asked Miss Marlowe the younger. "I should have thought Geneva — "

"Ah, it's on account of my aunt," said Julia swiftly. "She's taking the cure, and wanted me to be with her. She brought me up, and we don't expect her to be with us much longer. Do you know Yorkshire at all?"

They did not, so she told them a great deal about her early childhood in a bleak stone house set among purple moors. There was no doubt that Julia's imagination, unexercised now for six days, had fairly taken the bit between its teeth. Convincing details, picturesque episodes, sprang one after another to her lips. She was run away with by unbroken ponies; she was lost in sudden mists; she struggled through the snow to the rescue of a pet lamb. The Misses Marlowe listened entranced, and so did Julia. She was not lying, she was entertaining; and the entertainment was so good that the first sight of Aix took both her and her audience by surprise.

"How quickly we've come!" exclaimed the elder

lady, quite unconscious of flattery. "Where can we put you down?"

Julia hesitated. The geography of Aix was a blank to her, the only building she positively knew it to contain being the casino itself; and though there was now no real reason (the journey safely accomplished) why she should not boldly announce it as her destination, her artistic instincts rebelled. It was the pet lamb that worried them; it was all wrong to jump straight from a pet lamb to a casino, and Julia almost felt she owed her hostesses an apology. But the casino it had to be, for she dared not hesitate long; so devoted a mother could not possibly have forgotten where she was meeting her young.

"At the casino, please," said Julia. "How disreputable that sounds! But my aunt loves it."

"It's all right in the afternoon, my dear!" said Miss Marlowe with a smile. "No one plays till night."

### 3

At half-past four Mrs. Packett, who had spent an agreeable afternoon writing out recipes, emerged from her room and found Susan and Bryan still under the pines. Bryan was reading *Mademoiselle Dax,* Susan had a volume of Molière; as her grandmother approached she put it down and reached for the big cowbell that would summon Claudia with the tea.

"Where is Julia?" asked Mrs. Packett.

Bryan looked up.

"She said something about going for a walk. She's probably collapsed into a café."

"Dear me," said Mrs. Packett, considering the sun-baked hillside, "and there's no nice tea-shop nearer than Belley. I hope she won't be too tired."

Susan alone showed no anxiety as to her mother's whereabouts. She drank her tea, dipped into her Molière, and did not encourage conversation. It was one of her characteristics that when she did not wish to be spoken to, people rarely spoke to her: she had the faculty of wrapping herself in a cloak of silence, folded in which she courteously but firmly withdrew from society. "Packett in her cloud" was a familiar college expression; she was in her cloud now. But behind it her thoughts too were busy with the absent Julia.

"Why is it all so different?" wondered Susan. "We're here just as we used to be before she came, and yet it's all changed." A part of the change at least lay in the fact that she herself was no longer the un-disputed centre of their tiny society — that the attention of Bryan and Mrs. Packett, previously concentrated on herself alone, was now liable to stray in another direction; but of this she was not consciously aware. What she was aware of, though but vaguely, was a general relaxing, so to speak, of the moral atmosphere. She couldn't put her finger on anything definite; she only knew that it was becoming more and more difficult to brace Bryan up. This bracing of her suitor was a matter of great importance to her; she was extremely anxious that he should impress Sir William, not only with his keenness in love, but also with his keenness in his profession. She wanted to produce him as a coming young man — as he undoubtedly was, if only he would take a little trouble. . . .

"It all depends on the people he's with," thought Susan. She had too nice a sense of decorum to add, even mentally, that he was in bad company when he was with her own mother; but the thought crossed her mind that Julia must by now be rather tired of Muzin.

"If Uncle William's motoring to Paris," she observed casually, "Julia might like to go with him."

Mrs. Packett looked at her in surprise.

"Has she said anything about going so soon, dear?"

"No, but she'd have a lovely run. It's the only way to see the country."

"I thought she'd stay and wait for us," said Mrs. Packett. "I want to fly the Channel, and I'm sure she'd come with me if you don't care to."

Susan said nothing.

"She must be dreadfully hot if she's walking," added Mrs. Packett solicitously. "I do hope she's had some tea."

Susan said nothing to that either.

## 4

Well it was for Mrs. Packett's kind heart that her vision did not reach as far as the Place du Revard; for there, at that moment, stood Julia in the most deplorable state of heat and thirst. Aix was a howling wilderness to her: she had lost her five francs in five seconds, there were no millionaires (at least none unattached), and not a single coronetted car. She was too footsore even to go and look at the shops. She was so desperate that if the property-aspirin had been poison indeed she would quite possibly have taken it.

To make matters worse, she had just come upon a large café of the most superior kind; its broad *terrasse* was hedged from the pavement by a row of beautifully clipped bushes just as high as her chin; and over these, as she loitered by, Julia could not help seeing the throng of happy creatures inside. There were beautiful ladies in white hats, less beautiful males who were evidently going to pay for what the ladies consumed; and at the sight of so many drinks Julia's heart fainted within her. She needed a drink. She needed a drink badly. What with heat, disappointment and weariness, she felt as though she had never needed a drink before.

By the time she reached the end of the hedge, longing had turned to resolution. She had not only needed a drink, she was damn well going to have one.

Julia turned round and slowly retraced her steps. She was determined that if they put her in prison it should be for three Manhattans. But as she once more followed and looked over the bushes, it occurred to her that perhaps she needn't go to prison at all. Several of the tables were occupied by gentlemen alone, some obviously expectant, but one or two as obviously free, and over these last Julia ran an experienced eye. Her final choice was plump and middle-aged, a prosperous-looking Anglo-Saxon whose general sobriety of demeanour was relieved by a bright and roaming glance. By great good luck there was an empty table beside him, and towards it Julia now made her way.

She had two preliminary objects — an eye to catch, an eye to avoid. The first belonged to her neighbour, the second to the waiter; and she succeeded in both, for the *terrasse* was so crowded that an inactive client could easily escape attention, and Mr. Rickaby — such was the prosperous gentleman's name — had attention to spare. Julia had not been seated two minutes before their eyes met: her own gaze was the abstracted kind, so useful for forming a sound opinion before committing oneself, and she held it at least ten seconds before starting and turning away. But she soon fell into a reverie again, and naturally the same thing happened. When it had happened three times Mr. Rickaby spoke.

"Very slow service, isn't it?"

"Terrible!" said Julia, with an encouraging smile.

It encouraged Mr. Rickaby so much that he slewed round his chair till he was practically sitting at her table.

"Waiting for someone?" he asked.

Julia twisted her mouth and shrugged. Instinctively she had pitched on exactly the right line — a slightly mournful cynicism such as Mr. Rickaby would enjoy dispelling. She was almost certain that he was a man who liked to do good.

"What you want," said Mr. Rickaby, "is a drink." And without waiting for an answer — thus showing that he was also a man who knew his way about — he energetically hailed a waiter and ordered two Martinis.

"Thanks," said Julia indifferently. She felt it was still too early for a gleam of gratitude, so she turned three-quarter face — not profile, because of the plumpness under her chin — and stared into the distance, and let him have a good look at her. Mr. Rickaby evidently appreciated what he saw, for when the drinks came he at once stated his intentions.

"Our eyes have met," quoted Mr. Rickaby softly, "our lips not yet — here's hoping. You by yourself here?"

"At the moment," said Julia.

"But not for long," suggested Mr. Rickaby.

Julia shrugged her shoulders.

"I'm alone in Aix," she said; "I haven't any luggage, and I haven't a bean. So hope is just what I need."

The mingled pathos and bravery in her voice touched them both. Mr. Rickaby made sympathetic clucking noises, and in each of her own eyes (without any conscious effort) Julia felt a tear start. It *did* sound awful, put baldly like that. . . . The only thing was, was it too awful? Had it frightened him off? Just in case, Julia shifted a point farther from pathos and a point nearer to bravery.

"I'm a fool," she said gamely. "It's not really so bad as that."

"Poor little girl!" said Mr. Rickaby.

Julia's answering sigh was partly one of relief. It was O.K., she'd been quite right, he did like to do good. With a sudden flash of insight she saw him as

— 153 —

a man who liked his good times, but occasionally had trouble with his conscience, and as a man therefore to whom the combination of a good time with a Good Work would be a positive godsend. . . .

"Tell me all about it," said Mr. Rickaby. "Tell me how you came here."

"With Lucien," said Julia.

"Lucien?"

"The dress designer," said Julia. How, she could not tell, but this sinister figure had at that very instant sprung fully-fledged from her brain. Lucien, the designer . . . a man about fifty; tall, heavy, with narrow coffee-coloured eyes . . .

"Never heard of him," said Mr. Rickaby, evidently with pride. "Some dago chap?"

"Armenian," corrected Julia. "Lucien is just the trade-name."

"Armenian! My God!" said Mr. Rickaby.

Julia sighed her agreement.

"You can't trust them," she said sombrely.

"And he's left you planted here?"

Julia gulped.

"This morning — when we were leaving the hotel — there was another woman in the car . . . Someone he'd just picked up. A very tall ash-blonde, with dark eyebrows."

"I believe I've seen her about," said Mr. Rickaby.

For a moment Julia was quite startled by her own powers.

"Not that one," she said hastily. "This one had only turned up last night. . . . But there she was in the car, and of course I wouldn't stand it. I said so. And then — can you believe it? He simply drove off."

"No!"

"With my luggage in the back!"

There it was, a good, interesting, watertight story, and Julia felt justifiably proud of it. It accounted for everything, and it aroused in Mr. Rickaby the pleasurable sentiment of righteous indignation. The things he was saying about M. Lucien were hard but deserved. Nothing, Julia felt, was too bad for that devilish designer — especially when you thought how he treated his work-girls. For a moment in Julia's imagination there hovered a vision of dreadful Armenian excesses: for M. Lucien was by this time so real to her that she knew exactly what happened whenever he got a girl to stay late. But she pulled herself up; she wasn't going to risk a libel action; and her next cue was already overdue.

"Now tell me about *you*," said Julia earnestly.

Mr. Rickaby told her. His story was not nearly so colourful as Julia's, but it was the one she wanted to hear. He was alone at Aix, and finding it rather dull. He had been overworking — overdriven, said Mr. Rickaby — and his doctor had ordered a complete change. He was obviously suffering for someone to talk to, and within the next half-hour had told Julia all about the complicated negotiations (amalgamation of two men's-outfitting stores) which had led to his over-working and his presence at Aix. It was the sort of talk Julia was used to, and she knew so many of the right questions to ask that Mr. Rickaby conceived a very high opinion of her brains.

"You understand," he said at last. "You're an in-telligent woman."

"It's so interesting," said Julia modestly.

Mr. Rickaby slapped the table.

"There you are. You're interested *because* you're intelligent. Now my wife isn't interested at all. The fact of the matter is, she doesn't understand me."

From sheer force of habit Julia glanced at her watch. For several years she used to have a permanent bet with one of her girl-friends that every man you met said that within the first hour; the girl-friend had said no, within the first half-hour; and they used to get quite a lot of fun out of jockeying their opponents (so to speak) into position — Julia holding the declaration off, Louise trying to bring it on; and then whoever lost had to stand the other a lunch. Good old Louise! thought Julia, with quite a rush of affection; she hadn't thought of the girl for years, but it was queer how that well-remembered phrase brought her suddenly to life. Red hair, she'd had, and a way with the boys that nearly always ended in a row. . . .

"You've heard that before, I expect," said Mr. Rickaby, watching Julia's face. "But what's a man to say, if it's true?"

"That's just it," murmured Julia.

"I don't say I'm easy," pursued Mr. Rickaby fairly. "I dare say I'm a bit more complicated than most men. I like all sorts of things — good music, you know, and scenery. I've got — well, I suppose I've got ideals. But it takes a woman like you to understand."

Julia nodded. She had often pondered this question of why wives didn't understand when women like herself did; and the only conclusion she had reached was that to understand men — to realize the full value of their good streaks, while pardoning the bad — you had to know so many of them. Then when you came across one fellow who was a soak, for instance, you could nearly always remember another who soaked worse; and *he* in turn might have qualities of generosity or cleverness which raised him above a third man who was a teetotaller. But to know all that you had to have experience, and wives as a rule hadn't. They knew only one man, where women like Julia knew dozens; but then women like Julia rarely became wives. It was a rotten system, when you came to look at it. . . .

"I expect I've left something out," meditated Julia. Her thoughts glanced at Susan, then hastily looked away, just as her eyes would have looked away if Susan had actually appeared among the café tables.

"Where are you going to-night?" asked Mr. Rickaby suddenly.

Julia hesitated. The leading-on of Mr. Rickaby, enjoyable as it was, had been the result rather of habit than of design; and she had not yet visualized any definite issue to their encounter.

"I don't know. . . ."

"You must come to my hotel," said Mr. Rickaby firmly. "*I'm* going to look after you now."

She pressed his hand. She could hardly do less. And, in truth, she felt very kindly to him. A vicarious gratitude on behalf of that other Julia — the Julia who had been so shamefully used by M. Lucien — swelled her heart. But her brain remained clear.

"How can I?" she murmured. "Without any luggage?"

"I'll see to that too," said Mr. Rickaby. He was being princely, and he knew it. "We'll go shopping. We'll buy you a suitcase and some things to put inside. How's that?"

Julia was properly overcome; but her brain went on working.

## 5

Considering that she was a stranger to the town, Julia showed some address in getting to the lingerie-shop first. There was a leather-goods establishment directly in their path, but she got her escort past it by suddenly looking into his face and asking what she was to call him. "Bill," said Mr. Rickaby. "I couldn't call you Bill!" said Julia. "It's too ordinary." And by the time they had decided that she should call him Ronald, the suitcases were passed. The next danger-point was the actual threshold of the lingerie-shop, but here she was aided by her companion's own modest nature. "You'll wait outside?" said Julia; and did not even have to add that she wanted to give him a surprise. Mr. Rickaby simply took out his fat pocketbook and handed her a thousand francs.

"Do you know," he said, smiling at her, "you're an answer to prayer?"

"So are you," said Julia; and since those were the last words she ever spoke to him, it was just as well that they made him happy.

Once inside the shop she took the simple and straightforward line of asking the vendeuse whether there was a back way out. The vendeuse looked through the glass door at Mr. Rickaby, and smilingly said that there was. Julia then bought a pair of very nice garters, to get change, tipped the girl, and was shown out. In the street she asked the way to a garage, and there hired a car, for the sum of two hundred and fifty francs, to take her back to Muzin. It made an awful hole in the money, but she was still over seven hundred up.

6

It was curious that, after behaving in so perfectly ladylike a manner, Julia should have been troubled by her conscience. But so it was: as she sat comfortably in the car, her bag plumped out by Mr. Rickaby's notes, she could not help feeling — well, mean.

"He asked for it," she assured herself. "He was having a gamble, and he lost. I hope it'll be a lesson to him."

For some minutes this new view of her conduct — that she had been altruistically and deliberately showing Mr. Rickaby the folly of his ways — brought a certain comfort. But the comfort did not last. In spite of herself Julia could not help picturing him waiting and wondering, and then perhaps going into the shop, and making a fool of himself in front of the vendeuse, and then stamping out again with a hot and angry face. It was all part of the lesson, of course, but men did feel that sort of thing so. . . .

To cheer herself up Julia took out the new garters

— 160 —

and tried them on. They were black, with silver crescents. She hitched up her skirt and stretched out a shapely but solid leg, and found the effect extremely good. It was just at that moment that the chauffeur turned round to ask a direction.

"*C'est près de Belley, Madame?*"

"*Oui, oui,*" said Julia, letting down her skirt again.

"Yes, yes," said the chauffeur, grinning.

"You attend to your job," said Julia.

She was furious as much with herself as with him, and the incident ruffled her. If it had been Susan in the car he would never have dared. But then Susan wouldn't have been trying on garters. . . . "It's not that," thought Julia; "it's just something about me. They see they can take advantage, and they do. Mean, I call it."

Anger warmed her, and with the subconscious purpose of putting herself in the right, she directed it upon Mr. Rickaby. A man old enough to be her father — very nearly! "The old rip!" thought Julia. If she hadn't had the sense to come away, goodness knew what mightn't have happened! The idea that he was still at large in Aix, getting ready, no doubt, to entangle the next thirsty young woman who came his way, was quite distressing to her. She ought to have told the police about him. She ought to have given him in charge. He was a menace to female virtue, and it was no wonder girls went wrong. . . .

"All the same," murmured the voice of Julia's conscience — and oddly enough it was also the voice of red-haired Louise — "all the same, dear, you did lead him up the path. . . ."

Julia rapped on the glass and told the chauffeur to stop. They were just outside the village, and she had no wish to arouse unnecessary comment. When she gave the man his tip he did not touch his cap, but swept it off with a low bow; and though Julia was almost sure this was wrong, she dared not try to rebuke him. She had a strong presentiment that if she opened her mouth, it would be to swear.

## 7

The first person she met in the villa grounds was Bryan Relton. He at once came towards her with an exaggerated air of anxiety relieved.

"My dear Julia! Where on earth have you been?"

"For a walk," said Julia.

Mr. Relton looked at her thoughtfully, but did not ask where she had gone. Though Julia had no desire to be questioned, the omission for some reason annoyed her.

"Well?" she said sharply.

Mr. Relton continued to gaze.

"You look to me," he said pensively, "like a cat who's just eaten the canary."

Julia stared at him, speechless.

"And I don't believe," continued this most objectionably perspicacious young man, "that it's going to agree with you."

Julia just managed to get to her room, and then she did swear.

# Chapter 13

Whenever Julia, after a period of distress, found herself once more in funds, she gave a party; so on the next day, which was one of the villa shopping days, Mr. Rickaby played unwitting host to a second luncheon at the Pernollet. "Of course it's on me!" said Julia gaily; and for an hour and a half thoroughly enjoyed herself. At the moment of paying, however, she got a nasty jar.

"What a lovely clean note!" observed Susan idly.

Julia jumped. It *was* lovely, fresh and crisp as though it had just been drawn from the bank: a note for five hundred francs. It was hardly probable that Mr. Rickaby should have taken the number; but supposing he had — and suppose it ever got back to him — and supposing he had it traced . . .

"He'd never do anything," Julia assured herself, "He'd only think I must have a hell of an appetite. . . ." But as one fear was quieted another took its place; for the first time it struck her that Susan wouldn't be really pleased to know that Mr. Rickaby had paid for her lunch. Susan never would know, of course — but if she did! The thought turned Julia hot all over.

Aloud, and quite unconscious of the length of the pause, she said: "I got it in London. I hate dirty money."

"Filthy lucre," remarked Bryan — his tone as idle as Susan's, but his eyes alert. "Personally I shouldn't mind how filthy it was, so long as it paid for this lunch. For what I have received, the Lord knows I'm truly thankful."

Susan, standing by her chair waiting for Mrs. Packett to get up, opened her mouth and on a second thought closed it again. There was evidently a lecture impending, and Julia, to pay Bryan out, at once provided an opportunity for it.

"You young ones ought to walk back," she said firmly. "It's not too hot and the exercise will do you good."

"Yes," said Susan quickly. "I was just thinking the same thing. Ready, Bryan?"

He looked at Julia, met a stony glance, and resigned himself to the inevitable. As Julia followed Mrs. Packett into the car she saw the pair of them turn along the promenade and set off at an unnaturally brisk pace.

## 2

"Let's stop and have a bock," said Bryan, as they reached the big café.

"Why? You can't want one now, after all you had at lunch," said Susan reasonably.

"I don't want one, I should like one," explained Bryan.

Susan did not answer, but merely walked on. She was in no mood for frivolity. Bryan, glancing sideways, observed, and felt it a pity, that her profile was at its best when her mouth closed in that quiet inflexible line. How different a mouth from Julia's with its full lower lip and deep corners! How different from Julia altogether, this slim young Amazon who walked looking straight in front of her, with never an answering glance for the admiring looks commanded by her silver Anglo-Saxon colouring. If only the Julia in her — and surely so vivid a mother must in a daughter live again — could be brought out and allowed to flower! And as always, in the midst of his resentment, Bryan was at once tantalized and enchanted by the vision of a Susan not silvery, but golden; not cold, but warm; of a Susan whom he felt so capable of discovering and of bringing to life — if only the silver Susan would let him. . . .

"Why did you say that at lunch?" demanded Susan abruptly.

"Say what, darling?"

"About not caring how dirty the money was, so long as it paid for you."

Bryan grinned. He knew well enough why he had said it: to get a rise out of good old Julia, because he was morally certain that there was something fishy about that note. Although her previous afternoon's activities were in detail unknown to him, he had given, without the least loss of appetite, a surprisingly good guess at their general outline; but he also shared Julia's opinion that Susan would not be pleased.

"That! I don't know," he said lightly. "Just for the sake of saying something, I suppose."

"I wish you hadn't," stated Susan, frowning. "If you didn't mean it, it was just foolish; and if you did it was rather rotten."

"All right, I'm just a fool," agreed Bryan amiably. "Let's try going across-country." He wanted to get off the highroad, among trees, into the shelter of a hedge: he had the firmly-rooted masculine conviction that all female criticism was best met by kissing.

Rather to his surprise, Susan nodded. They turned aside, taking one of the lanes that wound to the right over a little hillock. On its summit rose the abandoned shell of a fine new villa; there was no water on that hilltop, as the impetuous architect had belatedly found out. "What an idiot he must have been!" thought Susan absently. She had no patience with people who leapt before they looked — who staked everything on a view, without considering the water-supply; and since she was now (so to speak) considering a water-supply herself, she did not respond to the pressure of Bryan's hand. She knew already that he could supply her with the view.

"You're not a fool," she said seriously. "And things like that — they worry me, Bryan. The things that slip out when you're not thinking."

He let go her hand and regarded the landscape with an air of exasperation.

"Darling, if you expect every word I say to be weighed in the balance first — "

"You know I don't. I should hate it."

" — or if you expect me to talk all the time as though I'm on oath — "

"I don't!" cried Susan again. "It's not that at all!"

"Then if you want to know," finished Bryan angrily, "I think you're making an absurd fuss over nothing."

They broke off, aghast. But to Bryan, who had often wished to provoke just such a scene, the moment was not without its compensations. He enjoyed, fiercely, the pleasure of letting his irritation get the better of him. He enjoyed Susan's wide gaze of distress, and the faint colour that stained her throat. Then the savage moment passed, and his heart dropped like lead.

"Susan — darling — "

"It's all right," said Susan quietly. She too had recovered herself; she could meet his imploring gaze with a smile. "Only — only if you feel like that, and I feel so differently, it seems pretty hopeless."

"Nothing's hopeless, if you'll stick to me," said Bryan urgently. He meant it. His penitence was so great that he felt capable of any sacrifice — more, of any long laborious toil — that would reinstate him in her graces. Susan turned away her head. To her also it was a moment for self-examination.

"I know Julia thinks I'm a prig," she said slowly.

"Damn Julia!"

For some reason Susan's expression immediately relaxed. Her next words came more easily, almost impetuously, as though a confidence withdrawn had been suddenly renewed.

"If I am, I shall be one all my life. That's what I want you to understand, Bryan: if you find me too — too difficult now, I don't believe I shall ever be easier. I can't pretend. I can't behave as though things aren't important, when I know they are. Things you think are too little to worry about. I've tried — it does sound priggish, and I know it — to set a guard about myself. . . ."

There was a long silence. They were both too much moved for speech; they were both suddenly humbled, Susan before the vision of a perfect integrity, a holiness of the mind, Bryan before the reflection of it through Susan. It was the deepest emotion he had known, and so strange to him that he could not understand, but only feel. His words, when at last they came, and inadequate as they were, had at least sincerity to strengthen them.

"You're the best thing there ever was, Susan. You make me feel one of the worst."

She reached out behind her — she was now walking a little in front of him — and felt for his hand. He took it and plunged on.

"You've got such hellishly — such heavenly — high standards. You — you'll have to haul me up to them."

"Can I, my dear?"

"If you want to, you know you can. Only — pull hard."

She drew him close beside her, and they finished their walk like lovers.

### 3

That night, for the first time since her arrival at Muzin, Julia was unhappy. She told herself three fortunes, and each was worse than the last: she was going to have trouble in old age, and be jilted by a fair stranger, and suffer disappointment in her plans. Nor was she in the least surprised, for everything was going wrong already. Her successful raid on Aix had produced totally unexpected consequences, and so had her scheme for the discomfiture of Bryan Relton. He and Susan had returned to the Villa trailing positive clouds of glory: they spent the whole evening walking up and down the terrace discussing his career. "It can't last," thought Julia; but when she looked at her daughter's face she almost doubted. Susan was so strong-minded! But even if she gained complete ascendency, if she managed to hold Bryan's nose to the grindstone and turn him into a pillar of the law, she couldn't change his nature. He might behave like a solid pillar for year after year, but one day he would crack, and then down would come all Susan's firmly-built house. "Perhaps it's that lunch," thought Julia, quite aghast at her own gloomy prescience. "Rich food never did agree with me. . . ." But she knew she was fooling herself; rich food as a rule was just what she throve on. However, she went to her room and took a sodamint, and either that or her long night's sleep did her good. She woke up still feeling melancholy, but only gently and sentimentally so; and since it was an instinct with her always to make the most of any emotion, she slipped out alone and bent her steps towards the ruined pavilion.

# Chapter 14

It was more dilapidated than Julia had thought — doubly so, indeed, for even the repairs were themselves in need of repairing. A sheet of zinc under the roof no longer kept out any but the mildest weather; in every wall long zigzag cracks split the superimposed plaster. There were seedlings between the boards, cobwebs under the beams; and the only elegant thing there was a little slender grey-green lizard that fled at Julia's step.

Her disappointment was great. She had hoped for true-lovers' knots, faded but still blue, perhaps even a cupid or so; especially she had hoped for some sign of recent occupation. A cushion, a letter, a mere heart scratched on the wall — any of these would have pleased and contented her. But there was nothing. There was not even a view, for the nut trees grew too close. "It's a shame!" thought Julia vaguely; her pity being half for anyone else who might be similarly disappointed, half for the pavilion itself. And the emotion (though vague) was not a barren one: with sudden resolution she took out her lipstick and drew a heart of her own.

Scarcely had she finished when a sound of voices below brought her hastily back to the doorway. There were people on the path, Susan and Bryan and a tall unknown man. He had grey hair, and as he walked his hand rested lightly and familiarly on Susan's shoulder. Susan looked up, even her height diminished by his, and smiled affectionately. Bryan, a little behind, was wearing his best deferential air. . . .

Sir William had come.

2

Julia now naturally wanted to get down unobserved and go back to the house and tidy her hair and come out again and be discovered in the garden; and as the path turned almost at once, she had every hope of being able to do so. But Bryan, already behind, let the others pass out of sight while he stopped to tie his shoe.

"*Sst!* Julia!" he hissed.

With as much dignity as she could muster, Julia advanced to the top of the steps.

"What are you doing there?" she asked severely.

"The question is, what are you? I spotted you as we

came up, and thought perhaps you weren't feeling social."

"I wasn't," said Julia crossly. "I'm not now. Is that Sir William?"

"It is, darling. The ranks of the godly are increased by one. Shall I help you down?"

But Julia refused his assistance and descended alone. She had no time to waste on foolishness.

"You go on with the others," she directed, herself taking the lower path. "I've an important letter to write."

"Hi! Julia!"

Simply to stop him shouting, she turned and looked back.

"What is it now?"

"When you've written your letter — and changed your frock — where would you like us to discover you?"

Julia had a very good mind to ignore the impertinence altogether. But she didn't.

"Under the pines," she said hastily; "and *not* for half an hour."


3

Exactly twenty-five minutes later she was in position. She had on a fresh white frock, and not too much lipstick. On her knee lay *The Forsyte Saga*. She wished for a dog, but the villa could not supply one, and Anthelmine's cats were too common-looking.

The minutes passed slowly while Julia held her pose. She was afraid to lean back, in case the seat should mark her dress; there were several deck-chairs, but the rustic bench had a suggestion of Marcus Stone which strongly appealed to her. As once before, on the lower terrace, Julia was acutely aware of herself as part of a charming picture. "There ought to be a man!" she had thought; and now that a man was imminent, her consciousness was correspondingly heightened. With straining ears she listened for the voices in the vineyard; and when at last they became audible they were so much closer than she expected that she had barely half a minute to become absorbed in her book.

To the party above she was now distinctly visible, and Susan called cheerfully down to her. Julia did not stir. She was going to look up with a start, but she was going to do it at close range. She just turned over a page and smiled slightly, as though at some cultured witticism.

"Hi, Julia!" cried Bryan, quite close at hand.

At that Julia started in earnest, for he had leapt the last bank and was speaking positively in her ear. She gave him one good glare, and turned with a welcoming smile for the more decorously approaching figures of Susan and their guest.

"This is Sir William — my mother," said Susan, also directing upon Bryan a repressive look. It was unfortunate for the young man that the return of his lady-love's favour at once produced in him those same high spirits which had been the cause of his losing it. As Susan said herself, she could not pretend; she could not pretend now to be pleased that he had leapt down that bank and made her mother jump into the air just as Sir William was about to be introduced. . . .

Julia, however, noticed none of this, being too much taken up with her own deportment. It was beautiful. She graciously inclined her head, graciously extended her hand, and by moving a little along the bench, invited Sir William to sit.

"Take a deck-chair, sir," suggested Bryan maliciously. "That thing's as hard as nails."

But Sir William sat down by Julia. He was tall and thin, sunburnt, with slightly rough grey hair and the kind of profile she most admired. An aquiline nose was one of her weaknesses, and Sir William's was a real beak. "Distinguished!" thought Julia, after her first discreet glance. "He could play an Ambassador just as he stands!"

"What a beautiful place this is!" said Sir William distinguishedly.

"Remarkable," agreed Julia. "Are you fond of scenery?"

Sir William said that he was. He added that as he had his car with him, he hoped to see a good deal of it. If the next day were fine, they might all motor up the Grand Colombier and have lunch on top. They would be able to see the Rhône and Mont Blanc.

"What kind is it?" asked Julia.

Since Sir William looked a trifle puzzled, it was perhaps as well that Bryan answered for him.

"Dark blue Daimler," he said succinctly. "I hope, sir, that barn doesn't leak?"

"I hope so too," replied Sir William with philosophy, "but any barn a Frenchman isn't using is pretty certain to be derelict. However, the weather seems settled enough."

Susan glanced up at the blue and white sky.

"The clouds are coming from the Midi," she said, "which isn't a very good sign. Julia's had the one perfect week this summer."

These last words, in conjunction with the disastrous fortunes she had dealt herself the night before, struck Julia as ominous. Could it be that the arrival of Sir William, to which she had so much looked forward, was to prove fatal to her peace and happiness in the character of young Mrs. Packett? Was he going to see through her, like Bryan, and — unlike Bryan — de-

— 177 —

nounce her and turn her out? His aquiline features, even in repose, looked terribly stern; what would they be like when agitated by righteous indignation? "Grand!" thought Julia involuntarily; for already she admired Sir William very much indeed. She was like a passenger in a small boat who, fearful of a storm, would nevertheless enjoy seeing the ocean rage. Sir William's wrath would be terrible, but it would be a fine sight. "I'm all right so far," thought Julia, summoning her courage. "I've just got to keep my head. . . ."

All through lunch, therefore, she said hardly a word. She wiped her mouth both before and after drinking, took no second helps, and was very attentive to Mrs. Packett. Bryan, after his momentary relapse, was on his best behaviour too, and almost equally silent. Susan and her grandmother talked to Sir William, asking after common acquaintances — several of them, to Julia's pleasure, with titles — and about his tour through France. But the meal as a whole was unusually dull, and no one sat long over coffee. Julia in particular was so exhausted that she went straight to her room and slept for two hours.

After tea Sir William took them all for a drive. Susan sat in front, Julia with Bryan and Mrs. Packett in the back. The car was a beauty, and they saw some very nice scenery. Then they came home and dined, and after dinner played bridge. Bryan (his behaviour was fluctuating like a fever-chart) suggested poker, but Julia felt herself bound to sit on him. "I hate gambling," she said virtuously, "I think it's so bad for the character"; so they played several rubbers, Mrs. Packett sitting out, at twopence a hundred. At half-past ten Susan yawned; at a quarter to eleven Julia revoked, and no one but Sir William noticed it. Then Claudia brought in the barley-water, and they all went to bed.

"I'm so glad Sir William has come," said Mrs. Packett to Julia, as they passed through the lobby on the way to their rooms. "It will make things a little gayer for you."

"Not half," said Julia grimly.

But she said it only to herself.

### 4

By next morning it was obvious that Susan's doubts had been justified; the weather was breaking, and the expedition to the Grand Colombier was by common consent put off. Julia was not altogether sorry; she had little desire to sit for another two hours — and possibly longer — cooped up with Bryan and her mother-in-law. Even in a Daimler, it wasn't worth it. The morning hours, however, now that their plan had fallen through, seemed unusually long; she would have liked to tell herself some more fortunes, but feared lest Sir William should see and despise her. He was wandering about rather aimlessly, now in the house, now in the garden; Susan had retired with her French, Bryan was nowhere to be seen, and Mrs. Packett, in the billiard-room, was busily engaged with what would probably turn out to be a small cookery-book. Julia looked in on her, and went hastily away. From the hall she caught sight of Sir William's tall figure on the porch steps. He was really beautifully set up! He had the straightest back, for his age, that Julia had ever seen, and for a moment she stood contemplating it with genuine pleasure. Then Sir William turned round, so quickly that she had no time to fall into an effective pose; and thus he too received an unexpected and attractive impression. For there was about Julia, when she forgot herself, a certain charming simplicity: she stood there admiring him with the happy candour of a child before a Christmas tree.

"Come up to the rock," invited Sir William, "and look for Susan's clouds."

"I don't mind if I do," said Julia. But her spirit, as she joined him, was wary. She was still rather afraid of his profile, and her anxiety to make a good impression almost tied her tongue. However, the opportunity was in many ways favourable; there was at least no Bryan to upset her with his too understanding looks, or with his overemphatic agreement whenever she made a cultured remark. . . .

"Do you care for Galsworthy?" asked Julia, as they began the ascent.

Sir William replied that he did. Which just showed — and Julia only wished that Susan had been there to hear.

"I've got *The Forsyte Saga*," she continued. "I think it's wonderful."

"A very fine piece of work," said Sir William. "Particularly *To Let*."

Since Julia had not yet reached that, this was rather a stumper. But she kept her end up well.

"*I* like *A Man of Property*. I think it's wonderful."

Sir William agreed with her again. Their conversation was not exactly animated, but it was of the most superior kind.

"Mrs. Packett looks remarkably well," said Sir William.

"Doesn't she?" said Julia.

It was surprising how soon a subject became exhausted. Julia, whose turn it now was, racked her brains in vain. There remained of course the whole great topic of Susan's marriage, but until she knew Sir William better — until her good impression had been made — Julia preferred to leave it untouched. He was too valuable an ally to be approached without due precaution.

"Do you like Aix?" asked Sir William.

"No, I don't," said Julia, taken unawares. "Not that I've ever been there," she added hastily. Sir William was too polite to notice the inconsistency, but the necessity for not noticing somehow killed that topic as well. They mounted for a while in silence, and soon Julia could not have spoken even if she had found anything to say. She needed all her breath to keep from panting. Sir William, with the privilege of his sex, frankly wiped his forehead; Julia made an effort to contract her pores. By the time they reached the foot of the rock her chief emotion was regret for her absent powder-box.

"Close, isn't it?" she gasped, as they came to a stand-still. She could feel the blood beating in her cheeks, the hair clinging to her temples: it would have astonished her to know that Sir William found the effect most attractive. "Florid," Mrs. Packett had written; "glowing," substituted Sir William; he thought that if only Julia would keep silent — or at any rate stop making genteel remarks — he could enjoy her company very much indeed.

"I love a nice view," said Julia, regaining her breath. She gazed raptly over the plain: clouds had drifted in over the encircling hills and lay like a canopy at a

level somewhat below their summits. Through great
ragged gaps, however, the sun still struck down, pick-
ing out here a village, there a little hill: Magnieu lay
in shadow, the roofs of Belley shone. Where, in all
that, was the Midi? wondered Julia; but she did not
care to show her ignorance by a direct question. Instead she asked what Sir William thought of the
weather.

"It's certainly unsettled," he told her, "but I haven't
Susan's local knowledge. If we do get a thunderstorm,
it'll be a big one. Shall you mind?"

"Not in the least," said Julia untruthfully. Thunderstorms were a terror to her, and if one happened in the
middle of the night, when she was all alone, she really
didn't know how she could bear it. Louise was just
the same — except that she, with the energy belonging
to her red hair, at least got some excitement out of
them: she used to rush out in her best nightgown
and have no end of a time. "I'd better put on my pink
satin," thought Julia. "I'd be too scared to change. . . ."
She shivered in anticipation.

"You're getting cold," said Sir William. "There's
more breeze up here than one thinks."

He turned to lead the way down, and Julia willingly
followed. It was lovely to have him hold aside the
branches for her, and give her a hand over the rough
places, but the necessity — as she conceived it — for

making polite conversation was still a dreadful worry. Sir William had apparently thrown up the sponge; they descended two thirds of the path in complete silence. At the turning under the pavilion, however, among the nut trees, an odd memory came into Julia's head, and she thoughtlessly gave it utterance.

"I had a little nut tree" —

recited Julia suddenly —

"And nothing would it bear
"But a silver nutmeg — "

She broke off, feeling rather foolish; but Sir William stood smiling at her.

" — And a golden pear," he finished. "You have a wonderful gift for completing the moment."

Julia didn't quite know what he was talking about, but she nevertheless felt flattered. Her spirits rose, and on a reckless impulse she said incautiously: —

"Do you know who taught me that? A Clown!"

"Circus or pantomime?" asked Sir William.

"Pantomime. When I was small, my mother used to play Columbine, and sometimes I waited for her in the dressing-room. And once, I don't know why, I was crying about something, and the Clown came in and took me on his knee and recited that about the nutmeg. It was ages before I found out that he hadn't made it up himself."

"And did it stop you crying?"

Julia hesitated. Since Sir William, for some reason, evidently thought highly of the rhyme, and since she herself thought highly of Sir William, she would have liked to say yes; but honesty forbade.

"I don't know," she confessed. "I *did* stop, but it was more likely because of the sausages. He let me play with them — and his poker."

"A Clown who recited nursery rhymes," said Sir William thoughtfully. "You must have had some wonderful stories to tell Susan."

Julia looked quite shocked. Tell Susan about her grandmother being a Columbine! What next! Fortunately the girl was not inquisitive, but should the question ever arise Julia had long made up her mind what to say. "Your grandmother on *my* side, dear, was the daughter of a clergyman." Which was quite possibly true, since Julia had never so much as heard her own grandfather mentioned; if she didn't know that he *was* a clergyman, she equally didn't know that he wasn't. . . .

Aloud she said, brusquely, "I've never told Sue anything. As I expect you know, I haven't been much of a mother to her."

"If you had," said Sir William, "you'd neither of

you be half what you are now." And irrelevantly, ab-
surdly, he quoted the rhyme again:—
> " . . . a silver nutmeg
> "And a golden pear."

"I don't know about you," said Julia, still put out,
"but I'm dying for a drink."

5

It would have taken more than barley-water (which
was all she got) to restore her equanimity. She had
accompanied Sir William into the vine for the sole
purpose of making a good impression on him; what
on earth had possessed her, then, to go gassing away
about Clowns and dressing-rooms? Why, with all the
beautifully correct present to draw upon, must she go
and dig up her peculiarly incorrect past? For he would
never have guessed, thought Julia fondly; if only she'd
held her tongue he'd still be taking her for a real lady.

She sat down to lunch in low spirits. It was just
as dull a meal as that of the day before—with this
difference, that besides being bored she was now nervous as well. She had a dreadful fear that Sir William
might say something about Clowns, or Columbines,
or even make some direct enquiry as to her early
career; and indeed his attempts at conversing with her
were alarmingly numerous. But Julia suppressed them

all. Even on the subject of Galsworthy she refused to be drawn. Galsworthy had written for the theatre, and theatres had Pantomimes, and Julia was taking no risks. After a while Sir William gave up trying, and devoted himself instead to old Mrs. Packett. At that Julia drew an easier breath, and by the time Claudia was clearing the meat-plates had recovered sufficient aplomb, and also sufficient appetite, to ask Susan what was the sweet.

"Harlequins!" said Susan gaily.

Julia started. Then surprise gave way to indignation as a most appalling thought flashed through her mind. He couldn't — he couldn't have told Susan *already?*

Susan's next words showed that he had not.

"The French for 'left-over,' I'm afraid, Uncle William. There's half last night's tart to be eaten, and a cream cheese."

Julia heard, comprehended, and felt her heart sink back into its proper place. But her peace was once more shattered, for across the table, in that moment, she had just caught Sir William's eye.

# Chapter 15

Julia's rôle as young Mrs. Packett now began to present greater difficulties than ever. It had been tricky enough at first — with Bryan always giving the wrong cue, Susan on the look-out for slips, Mrs. Packett perpetually trying to introduce a sub-plot; but the presence of Sir William, as Julia at once perceived, was going to make everything ten times worse. He was as dangerous as Bryan, as observant as Susan, and would quite likely take an interest in the cakes. To crown all, Julia was very much attracted by him.

"I would be!" thought Julia glumly.

For the first time in her life the prospect of a new sentimental encounter — with its delicious alternations of hope and despair, its exciting approaches to intimacy, and hardly less stimulating checks — gave her no pleasure. She hadn't the time for it. She needed all her wits, all her energy, simply to keep her end up. Her only hope, and she knew it, was to lump Sir William with the rest and make no attempt at individual attention.

For she had nothing to fear from him; though he might catch her out as often as Bryan did, he wouldn't give her away. Quite likely, now that they'd settled down again, he'd just stop taking any notice of her at all.

Unfortunately, Julia felt that if he didn't take notice of her she wouldn't be able to bear it.

Just at this time, as if in sympathy with her distress, the weather broke. Julia looked out at the streaming skies and for a moment took pleasure in the general desolation. Then she turned away disgustedly; it simply meant that they would all be cooped up indoors at closer quarters than ever. There was no ground so favourable to love affairs (someone had once told her) as a country house on a wet day; and one horn of her dilemma was accordingly sharpened. To avoid it Julia felt she would have gone on a walking-tour in the Sahara. Then Sir William shut himself up in his room with a quantity of papers, and Julia prayed for fine weather to bring him out again. She was in the most uncomfortable state of mind she ever remembered; and still it went on raining.

It rained and rained. Anthelmine the cook, stumping up from the village under a vast umbrella, announced that it was going to last. She was in a bad temper — the umbrella, though vast, had not been vast enough for her — and dinner accordingly suffered. It rained

all night, and all the next day. Even indoors, with
the windows shut, one could not for a moment forget
that it was raining. The sight could be shut out, but
not the sound; and to the steady drumming of water
on foliage the indomitable crickets added a fife ob-
bligato. No one ventured out save Susan, who put on
a mackintosh and went for a long walk. Bryan was
invisible at the lodge, Sir William stayed in his room
till water came through the roof, then wandered into
the hall and met Julia, who at that moment happened
to be taking the line of resistance. She at once bolted
back into her own apartment, and Sir William retired
to the billiard-room and Mrs. Packett.

The old lady was getting on better than any of them,
for she had one inexhaustible resource. Whenever she
had nothing else to do, she wrote letters. She was
never at a loss for a correspondent, never at a loss for
matter; all she needed was paper and ink; and the
result was rather like planchette-writing, disjointed
yet unhesitating. She put down, in fact, whatever came
into her head, and since her head was at that time
full of Julia's cake-shop, the news of this project
was being rapidly spread to the four corners of the
earth.

It will be, I think, in Kensington [wrote Mrs. Packett,
to a cousin by marriage who was in Australia], as Susan
tells me a great many people there are forced to live in

flats. Julia herself is not so certain about this, but we shall have a *good look round* when we all get back to town. You will know I am not *touting,* as you live so far away; but whenever you come home, my dear, I shall certainly take you for a nice cup of tea. . . .

The only event of the morning was the arrival of a second postcard from Fred Gennochio. "Glad you're enjoying yourself," it said. "All the best, Fred." But what touched Julia chiefly was the picture of Notre Dame. It was so beautiful and refined that she left it lying in the hall in the hope that Susan would see; and when Susan made no comment Julia went and fetched it out again to show to Mrs. Packett. The old lady admired it very much, and under the impression that it was for herself turned it over and read the other side.

"Fred?" she said enquiringly. "Surely not Fred Trevelyan?"

"It's for me," said Julia hastily; "it's from a friend of mine" — and involuntarily glanced over her shoulder to see whether Sir William had heard. After that she was so annoyed with herself that she went back to her room and watched the rain from there.

About four o'clock Bryan arrived from the lodge, complaining that he had lunched off rancid cheese.

"Then why didn't you come here?" asked Susan, whose six-mile walk had left her in a kindly, reasonable frame of mind that was highly irritating to the rest of the party.

"Because I didn't want to get wet, darling," said Bryan, shaking the water from his coat. "I may be English, but I'm not mad."

"It's raining just as hard now," pointed out Susan. "Would you like a hot bath?"

"No, I wouldn't," said Bryan. "And it's hardly raining at all."

After that they played bridge for several hours, until Mrs. Packett observed frankly that it was a game very trying to the temper. After that they all went to bed. Julia looked at her best satin nightgown, which she had been wearing in case of thunderstorms, then thrust it back in the drawer and put on a pair of cotton pyjamas.

## 2

Precisely at three o'clock the first mutter of thunder rolled round the hills and died away. The next crash sounded directly over the roof, and a glare of lightning lit the windows. Julia woke up, not quite aware of what had happened, and lay a moment wondering at the silence. The rain had almost stopped, not a cricket was to be heard. She got up to look out, and was halfway across the room when the thunder spoke again, almost petrifying her with fear. Oblivious of her pyjamas, conscious only of the need for human companionship, she ran to the door and out into the lobby. It felt safer there, less exposed, for the one window was tightly shuttered. Julia looked at the door opposite and wondered whether Sir William had been flooded out. If he had, he was doing nothing about it; within the house all was still. "They don't care!" thought Julia bitterly. "For all they mind I might die of fright!" Never before, not even on the first morning in the bath, had she felt so utterly lost, so completely isolated, so much a stranger under that hospitable roof. She took a few steps towards Mrs. Packett's door, then paused; that strong-nerved old woman was probably sound asleep, or else sitting up distracting her mind with recipes for shortbread. And Susan — Susan would be worse: sympathetic, no doubt, but faintly surprised that anyone she knew could be so chicken-hearted. . . . "There's no one!" thought Julia wretchedly. The thunder rolled, and she found herself once more outside Sir William's door. In spite of the heavy atmosphere she was shivering from head to foot; a great wave of despair, a premonition of unhappiness swept over and shook her. She could not move, she could only stand there, her shoulders pressed against the wall, waiting for the next thunderclap.

It came at last, but from a greater distance, and followed by an appeasing, steady downpour that was the

last of the rain. Julia pulled herself together, and crept
back to bed.

## 3

At half-past six next morning, in brilliant sunshine,
Bryan was on the lower terrace under Susan's window
throwing up gravel. The second handful brought her
head out, and some of the pebbles as well.

"Stop it!" she called. "It's going all over my bed!"

"Sorry," said Bryan, dodging the shower. "I tried
with roses, but they're so rotten to throw. Are you all
right, darling?"

"All right? Of course I am. Why shouldn't I
be?"

"I thought you mightn't have liked the storm very
much. I nearly came over to hold your hand."

"Thank goodness you didn't," said Susan practically.
"The front door was bolted and no one would have
heard you. What time is it?"

"Half-past six, and the most heavenly morning ever.
Come out and smell it." He suddenly advanced and
stood close under her window; it was so low that by
reaching up his fingers he could touch the sill. "Jump,
darling! I'll catch you!"

Susan laughed.

"You idiot! I'm only in pyjamas!"

"What the hell does that matter? There's no one

about. Put on some slippers and a coat if you like, only mind you don't catch on the creeper."

Susan's golden head — so bright, so charming — abruptly withdrew.

"I'll be out of the front door in five minutes," she called. "Go and get some proper shoes and we'll climb the rock."

For a minute Bryan stood where she had left him, looking down at his sandalettes. They were soaked through, and so, as far as the knee, were his tan-coloured trousers; for he had plunged straight up to the villa without using the path. He looked down at his feet, up at Susan's window; then turned, took a running jump on to the terrace wall, changed feet like a hunter, and flung himself down into the long grass. It was soaking, and he rolled in it. The sun was hot, the raindrops were icy, the double sensation made him want to shout aloud. But he restrained himself. Susan hadn't come when he wanted her, now let her see if she could find him. . . .

But Susan never thought to look in so damp a place.

### 4

One odd result of Sir William's arrival was that the burden of Julia's ill-got gains, which she had hitherto carried without much distress, became suddenly an intolerable weight. She could not understand it herself: she knew only that the remaining four hundred francs or so weighed like lead both in her handbag and on her heart. Such a state of affairs could not continue, and in the heat of the afternoon, while everyone else was resting, Julia retired to her room and there made sacrifice to an unknown god.

It would have looked better — a lot better — had she been able to return the whole amount; but no doubt Mr. Rickaby would understand. The notes, folded in a half-sheet of paper, made at any rate a respectable wad. Julia looked at them fondly, but her hand did not falter as she addressed an envelope to the Beau-Site Hotel. The idea of writing a letter was also present in her mind; it seemed so unfriendly just to return the money without a single word; but a letter might lead to an answer, or even to the appearance of Mr. Rickaby himself, and for that she had no desire. In the end she took a pen and wrote simply "From a Well-wisher" — to which the pen by itself added a couple of crosses. Then she licked down the envelope and was unfortunately compelled to steal one of Susan's stamps.

"All in a good cause," thought Julia cheerfully.

It was a hot day, but as a final penance she determined to walk into Magnieu and catch the afternoon post.

The village lay dozing under a sunlight that made

her blink. Its inhabitants were all in the fields, and their poultry kept house for them, walking in and out over the thresholds like neighbours paying calls. In a basket at the carpenter's door slept five particoloured kittens: their soot-black mother, one yellow eye open, lounged on the windowsill above. All was quiet — so quiet that Julia instinctively muffled her tread, stepping on the patches of straw that made sunshine even in the shade; but neither the poultry nor the cats took any notice of her.

She crossed the square with the fountain and took the Magnieu road. Like the village, it was deserted, and before she had gone far Julia began to feel as though she were the only person moving over the whole map of France. The sensation was disagreeable to her; she had a distaste for being alone with so much landscape. On her right, the breadth of a field away, towered a tree-covered bluff, brilliantly green against a sky brilliantly blue; both tones were as bright and as flat as if a child had painted them out of a new paintbox. To the left stretched the cultivated plain, more varied in colour, but robbed of all subtlety by the downright strength of the sun. Julia's sense of the theatre demanded a good-sized cloud or two, or at least a change of lighting; and she began to fix her eyes on a row of poplars that would presently break the monotony of the shadeless road.

Just before she reached it, however, the monotony
was broken in a different way. From close beside her,
but on the other side of the hedge, came the sound of
a slight scuffle, then a half-laughing, half-angry fem-
inine protest; and out of the next gate ran one of the
village girls. She had the attractive local face — pale-
skinned, blue-eyed — but also the less attractive local
figure; at the sight of Julia she hesitated, then marched
across the road into the field on the other side. Julia
continued on her way, and thus reached the still-swing-
ing gate at precisely the moment when Bryan Relton
came through it.

"Well!" said Julia.

With great presence of mind he turned round and
waved a hand towards the bluff.

"Grand view," he said, "but too damned hot."

"You've been kissing that girl," accused Julia.

"What girl?"

"The one who bounced out just now. You can't put
a view across me."

Bryan grinned.

"You're right, darling. You always are. But I couldn't
help it; I'd never kissed a cowherd's daughter before."

This was an attitude which Julia could well understand; but she thought of Susan and frowned.

"You oughtn't to do it," she said severely. "What
was it like?"

"Overrated," said Bryan, falling into step beside her. "And how much better to have found out! Now there's one sort of girl I shan't want to kiss again."

"You oughtn't to want to kiss any sort except Susan."

"I don't — in theory."

"Susan expects theory and practice to be the same."

"But then Susan is perfect, and I'm not."

"I know that," said Julia. She paused. "Perhaps I ought to have told you that I knew your father."

Bryan stared.

"The deuce you did! In — er — which capacity?"

"What d'you think?" asked Julia. "I don't know what he was like at home, but in a dressing-room he was a fair caution."

"And the sins of the fathers," quoted Bryan, "shall be visited on the children. So you've been holding *him* up against me too, Julia?"

"No, I haven't. I know how little difference it can make: look at me and Susan. I'd have felt the same about you if your father'd been a bishop."

They walked on in silence for another hundred yards, keeping close under the hedge to give room to an approaching ox-wain. When it had passed, at the next gate, Bryan came suddenly to a stop.

"Does it ever occur to anyone," he asked, leaning with his back to the post and his hands in his pockets, "that I may one day get a little tired of being constantly discussed and lectured?"

Julia bit back the obvious retort. She had a strong feeling that this was the mood most favourable to her own wishes.

"You'll be lectured a lot more before you're through," she said cheerfully. "Are you coming with me to the Post Office, or are you going to sulk?"

Bryan considered.

"I think I should like to get tight," he said simply. "I'll come with you to Magnieu and get tight there. There'll just be time to sleep it off before dinner."

"If there's one thing I hate," said Julia, "it's showing-off. You'll go straight back to the villa now, or — or I'll tell Susan of you."

He went. With one hurt, resentful look he turned on his heel and departed, while Julia continued along the Magnieu road. It was her first attempt at blackmail, and — unlike Mr. Rickaby's money — it did not trouble her conscience at all.

# Chapter 16

It was now a fortnight since Julia had had her hair washed. Being dark, she could go three weeks and still look presentable; but since the arrival of Sir William, and in spite of her determination to ignore him, presentability was not enough. She wanted a good close set, and plenty of brilliantine; and after a vain attempt to draw information from Claudia (whose own style dated from 1890) Julia went looking for Susan in the garden and interrupted her morning French.

"Where do you get your hair washed, Sue?"

"Here? I do it myself," said Susan.

Julia looked at her daughter's head — smooth, golden, with a slight natural wave — and smiled enviously.

"You *can*, of course. But me with my perm'! I'd never get it set. I suppose there's a hairdresser in Belley?"

"Two or three," agreed Susan. "I'll ask about them to-morrow, if you like, when we go in shopping."

"I'd rather get it done to-day," said Julia unreasonably. She had no ground for supposing Sir William more observant than most men, but he was always so beautifully spruce himself — as she had, at that very moment, an opportunity to note. For Sir William had joined them, appearing on the terrace just in time to catch Julia's last words.

"Anything I can do for you?" he asked.

"It's my hair," said Julia. "I want to get it washed. I think I'll have to try Belley."

"I'll run you over in the car," said Sir William.

Julia beamed with gratification. He really must like her, then! Because as a rule men hated a hairdresser's, it made them wait about . . .

"You won't have time before lunch," observed Susan practically. "It's nearly half-past twelve now."

"We'll have lunch at Belley," said Sir William. "We'll drive in, make an appointment, have lunch, and then Julia can get it done. How's that?"

"Perfect!" gasped Julia, quite overwhelmed by the magnitude of the offer. Then she looked quickly at her daughter, to see whether Susan wanted to come too. But Susan's air, as she returned to her books, was one of amiable relief only; she seemed sincerely glad to have got her parent fixed up.

"We'll now leave Susan in peace," said Sir William. "I'll have the car out in five minutes."

## 2

A happy woman was Julia as she took her place in the Daimler. To be seated by a Knight, in a large car, was almost her ideal of earthly bliss; with a good lunch in front of her as well, she felt that life had nothing more to offer. And her face showed it; she beamed with pleasure.

"Comfortable?" asked Sir William.

"Heavenly!" breathed Julia.

She adored him. She had always admired him as the most distinguished man she had ever seen, but her adoration dated from that moment. Something in that one word — the way he said it, smiling, but with his eyes fixed on the road ahead — went straight to her heart. Other words had gone straight to her heart before, but never with such force.

"Tell me if you want a cushion," said Sir William. "There's one behind."

Julia smiled. Since he was not looking at her, a smile was no answer; but she dared not speak. By some miracle she had made a good impression on this superlative man; the nerve-racking part was that she had no idea how she had done it. She could not tell now, for instance, whether he would like her to move up close, so that their shoulders touched, or whether he would prefer her to keep her distance. She stole a side-

ways glance at his thin aquiline profile; it had such
an effect on her that she had to look hastily away.

"I believe this is *it*," thought Julia uneasily. "I believe
this is the real thing. If I don't look out, I shall be
making a fool of myself."

Her thoughts raced on, and Sir William would have
been greatly surprised at them; for by the time they
reached Belley Julia had already dedicated herself to
a life of hopeless devotion. The prospect did not depress
her as much as might have been expected; it rather
thrilled her, and gave her a good opinion of herself.
It also gave her an immediate object, for with so many
sleepless and tearful nights ahead, it was absolutely
essential that she should have a photograph for the
tears to fall on.

"I should think you take wonderfully," she said, at
last breaking the silence.

"What, photographs? I don't know," said Sir William. "I haven't been taken for years."

Julia was slightly dashed. If she made him get taken
specially, he might think she was — well, interested in
him. And she didn't want that; her adoration was to
be unknown, unrequited, of the highest possible quality.

"I've some snaps taken on the *plage* at Cap-Martin,"
added Sir William, drawing up outside the Pernollet.
"They make me look like a scarecrow."

"I like men to be thin," said Julia. But she said it

with great detachment, so that it sounded like a general reflection only. "You should see the old geezers here — they're like a lot of pineapples."

Sir William laughed.

"The Pernollet is their only distraction. Live here a month or two yourself, and you'll see the danger."

"I wouldn't dare," said Julia seriously. "I've got to be careful. This evening I shall eat hardly anything at all."

"Then you'd better have a good lunch," he said.

### 3

Julia entered the restaurant with a proud and buoyant step. She did not walk, she swept. With Sir William behind her, and the Daimler outside, she felt the equal of any Disgusted Lady there. But her triumph was short; she swept only three paces; on the fourth she faltered. For the first person she saw, at a table directly in their path, was Mr. Rickaby.

Even at that peculiarly unfortunate moment Julia's first thought was an unselfish one: she was glad to see that he had consoled himself. For Mr. Rickaby was not alone, he had a companion, a handsome blonde with a good-humoured face; just the thing for him, thought Julia, as Mr. Rickaby no doubt was just the thing for *her*. Then, as the thought flashed through her mind, Mr. Rickaby glanced up.

"There's someone who knows you," said Sir William.

Julia turned round to deny it, and saw that he was looking in an opposite direction. At a table to their right sat the two Misses Marlowe.

There was nothing to do but smile and nod back, and this Julia did with admirable aplomb. Standing half the restaurant away she felt reasonably safe; she was even pleased that they should see her in the distinguished company of Sir William. So Julia smiled and nodded with her best Packett air.

It was also necessary — which Julia had not realized — to pass directly alongside their table. A beckoning *maître d'hôtel* left no option. The Misses Marlowe smiled again; the elder, who had been much taken by their new acquaintance, even put out her hand in a friendly and detaining gesture.

"We meet again!" she exclaimed cordially. "Did you find your children waiting for you?"

With the small of her back (as though she had suddenly developed a new nerve there) Julia distinctly felt Sir William's start of surprise.

"Yes, of course I did," she mumbled hastily. "Of course . . . Thank you very much."

"Perhaps we may all meet at Aix," elaborated Miss Marlowe. "And then you must show them to us." Her keen old eyes, as she spoke, glanced over every inch of Sir William's long figure: she evidently took

him for Julia's husband, and was as evidently prepared for an introduction. But Julia, with one more
incoherent mutter, passed quickly on; and a moment
later found herself seated opposite Sir William's
placid but enquiring gaze.

"Go on, you order the lunch," she said. "I'll tell
you when I've had a drink."

"Don't if you'd rather not," said Sir William politely.

But Julia had to. She felt she couldn't sit opposite
him for an hour, or maybe longer, with the shadow
of an unexplained family hanging between them.
As soon as the lunch was ordered, and their *apéritifs*
consumed, she took the plunge.

"Those," said Julia (and the plunge was indeed a
very little one), "are two ladies who live at Aix."

"I should think extremely nice acquaintances," said
Sir William.

"Aren't they?" agreed Julia, gratified, even in the
midst of her distress, at having given cause for his
slightest approval. An odd cause it was too, when
you came to think of it; and Julia thought so long
that at last Sir William had to prompt her.

"I'd an idea they seemed interested in me as
well?"

"They were," said Julia. "That's just it." She drew
a deep breath. "I think they thought you were the

— 207 —

father of my three children. Elizabeth, and Ronald, and — and I've forgotten the other one's name . . ."

To her extreme amazement, to her no less extreme relief, Sir William, after a moment's astonished silence, put back his head and laughed until the arrival of the *pâté*.

After that they got on famously. Julia did not tell him everything, of course, — she suppressed Mr. Rickaby altogether, and substituted for her desire to visit the casino a simple desire for a jaunt, — but she told him all about her assault on the Daimler, and most of the lost-sheep-and-heather stories with which she had beguiled her hosts. Sir William seemed to find them extremely entertaining, and as her confidence grew Julia proceeded to other and equally picturesque episodes of her past life. For the first time since her arrival in Muzin she was completely herself; she had cast all care aside, she no longer bothered even about being a lady. A glorious ease flooded her soul; mentally and physically she had her elbows on the table. For Sir William wasn't being shocked, he was being thoroughly amused; he was *liking* her, enjoying her company, just as though he'd been one of the boys and not a Knight at all. If the Packetts could only see them . . .

"Gosh!" cried Julia. "You won't let out any of this to the others?"

"Of course I won't, if you don't want me to," promised Sir William. "But why not?"

"Why not!" Julia's round dark eyes widened with astonishment. "Because — because they think I'm a lady!"

"And so you are," said Sir William.

She loved him for it, but she knew it was only his niceness.

"Not really. Not their sort. I'm not *vulgar,* but I've got to be careful. In fact — and in a way I'm glad to tell you — Bryan's seen through me already."

At that Sir William's brows came down, and all at once he looked like a Knight indeed.

"That young man!" he said grimly. "If he's been impertinent to you — "

"He hasn't," cried Julia. "It's just that he's a bit the same sort — And that's another thing: that's why he mustn't marry Susan. I couldn't tell you before, because I didn't want to give myself away. But you don't think she ought to marry him, do you?"

"To tell you the truth, my dear," said Sir William surprisingly, "I haven't thought much about it. I'm fond of Susan, of course, and I should see she didn't get tied up to a blackguard; but I've never found her particularly interesting."

It has been remarked before that Julia's maternal instinct was highly erratic. One minute earlier such

an offhand dismissal of her marvellous daughter
would have roused her to fury: she would have glared
like a tigress, and like a tigress sprung; but two words
from Sir William had, within the last few seconds,
changed all that. He had called her "my dear"! — and
those two words had so violently impinged upon her
heart, and had so largely printed themselves there,
as to confuse all previous inscriptions. Julia still loved
her daughter, but she adored Sir William; and she had
no idea of quarrelling with his judgment.

"I came to the villa," continued Sir William, thoughtfully, "purely from a sense of duty. But I'm very
glad I did."

"Oh, so am I!" said Julia.

It was just at that moment that Mr. Rickaby and
his friend, making for the door by a circuitous route,
passed close beside the table. He saw Julia, and Julia
saw him; out of the fullness of her glad heart she
gave him a hearty smile. It was irresistible in its
warmth and friendliness, and Mr. Rickaby smiled
forgivingly back. The last wrinkle in Julia's conscience was smoothed out; she left the restaurant at
peace with all the world.

The rest of the afternoon passed like a beautiful
dream. They went for a long drive — but not into
Aix — and Julia talked all the way. They stopped
for tea at a peculiar little inn where the *patronne,* who

served them, observed frankly that she had a very nice bedroom; and Sir William did not mind. "It's me," said Julia, with a frankness at least equal; she was very anxious for Sir William's dignity. She had already determined that if by any marvellous chance he asked her to go away with him — he wouldn't, of course, but just supposing he did — she would try and behave exactly like a wife.

They got back to the villa just in time, as Susan informed them, to change for dinner. The sight of her daughter roused Julia, as always, to heartfelt admiration; but it occurred to her as strange that she and Sir William, having been summoned all across France to Les Sapins solely by the question of Susan's marriage, should have found there something of so much greater interest.

### 4

"Did you find a nice hairdresser?" asked old Mrs. Packett at the dinner table. She was rather short-sighted, and the question was quite without malice; what disturbed Julia more was the fact that both Susan and Bryan, who were not shortsighted at all, had preserved a discreet silence.

"No, I didn't," said Julia brazenly. "They were all horrid. I'll have to try Aix."

# Chapter 17

The trip to Aix took place, but Mrs. Packett came too. Julia did nothing to stop her, and even welcomed her company, for she was extremely anxious that the new relationship between herself and Sir William should not attract notice. She dreaded Bryan's sharp eyes and sharper tongue — not so much on her own account as on Sir William's; she could not bear the thought of causing him even a moment's embarrassment. Rather than jeopardize a morsel of his dignity, she set herself a Spartan programme of self-repression; no one was to guess that she was the least in love.

How difficult a task that was! For Julia loved with enthusiasm. She put all her heart into it. She longed to show, by her manner, by her voice, by her every action, that she regarded Sir William as the nonpareil of humanity. Flying (as usual) to extremes, she attempted at first a mask of complete indifference, and refused to take part in an expedition to the Colombier; with the result that everyone at the villa immediately assumed that she was not feeling well. Mrs. Packett suggested an aspirin; Susan advised a good stiff walk and offered her company, which alarmed Julia so much — she had a vision of herself being made to tramp for three hours up a hill — that she rapidly resumed her normal habits. These now seemed to include a good many morning tête-à-têtes with Sir William in the garden. Julia erroneously fancied that they would pass either unmarked, or as common politeness to a guest at a loose end.

Her first warning, oddly enough, came from Anthelmine the cook. Since Sir William's arrival there had been no more games of patience, and Anthelmine evidently missed them, for every now and then she would come out of her kitchen, take a look under the pines, and stump gloomily back. Julia had pointed this out to Sir William, and made him laugh at the explanation; afterwards she wished she hadn't. For Anthelmine, it appeared, began to find something under the pines even more interesting than patience; whenever Sir William and Julia were there alone she came more frequently than ever. Sometimes, benevolently, she brought them out titbits — a plate of plums, or some newly baked *petits fours;* oftener she came simply to have a look. And Anthelmine's looks were in a class by themselves — so frank in their enquiry, and, as the days went by, so frank in their congratulation, that Julia did not know how to meet them. At last she made Sir William carry a couple of chairs to the second terrace in the vine; but even thither Anthelmine followed (with some fine radishes) and made matters worse by addressing Sir William in French.

"What did she say to you?" asked Julia nervously.

"'Gather ye rosebuds while ye may,'" replied Sir William; "but this is a long way for her to climb."

After that Julia saw she must be more careful; but it was already too late. Although, by exercising the sternest self-control, she had managed to conceal about three quarters of her sentiments, her adoration of Sir William was now so immense that the remaining fourth was enough to rouse Bryan's suspicion.

"What's the French for 'love nest'?" he asked Susan. "*Nid d'amour?*"

Susan, who happened to be doing a prose exercise at the moment, automatically put out her hand for the dictionary, and stopped halfway.

"I shouldn't think so," she said seriously. "Slang's awfully hard to translate. Why do you want to know?"

"So that I can write it up on the gate; it's time this place was rechristened. Darling, you don't mean to tell me you haven't noticed?"

"Noticed what?"

"Julia and Uncle William, of course. Our new romance."

"Nonsense," said Susan sharply.

"Not nonsense at all, darling. They're practically never out of each other's sight."

Susan laid down her pen and frowned.

"Uncle William's simply being nice to her, as I asked him to, and of course Julia enjoys being taken about. I wish you wouldn't talk like that, because it's so silly."

Bryan sat down on an open copy of Racine. The emotions he had aroused were quite incomprehensible to him; it struck him for the first time that Susan, like Queen Victoria, had a remarkable capacity for not being amused. Damn it, it was amusing — or at any rate highly interesting! — to see the distinguished and decorous Sir William fall so heavily for good old Julia. . . .

"She must be such a thorough change," he mused aloud. "I wonder if she calls him Bill?"

"I loathe gossip," said Susan suddenly. "You're just like the women at college who rush round saying 'Did you see So-and-so having coffee with Someone Else?' It — it — "

"I know," said Bryan. "It lowers the dignity of human nature."

Susan looked at him with surprise.

"Yes. Then if you see that, why do you do it?"

"Perhaps because I haven't got a particularly high opinion of its dignity to start with. On the other hand, I think a great deal of it as an entertainment."

"And that's all?"

"That's all," agreed Bryan cheerfully.

The next moment, at the sight of Susan's face, he was on his knees beside her.

"Except you, my darling! You're the only thing that matters! You're everything to me, Susan — the whole world!"

But even as he said it, as he felt her hands tighten round his head, he couldn't help wondering whether that was the sort of thing Sir William said to Julia.

2

So far, at any rate, it was not. The new romance was proceeding along such highly unorthodox lines that Sir William, whenever he got Julia alone, spent most of his time laughing. Their luncheon at the Pernollet had put her completely at ease with him; she said whatever came into her head, introducing, without scruple, a horde of old acquaintances, and seasoning her discourse with bons mots culled admittedly from the Bodega. And Sir William was worthy of her confidence: the recurrent figure of Mr. Macdermot, for instance, seemed to arouse no unusual curiosity, and he never once enquired why it was that Julia, with her secure income, had been so patently living from hand to mouth. This last point struck Julia so forcibly, and impressed her so much, that she made a clean breast of the whole business.

"*They* don't know, of course," she said anxiously, "and that's the worst part. How can I keep a cake-shop, when I haven't a bean?"

"You mean you haven't *anything*?" asked Sir William, to whom such a situation, in a person almost connected with him, was naturally startling.

"Not a cent," said Julia thankfully — for it would have been dreadful to answer that question with Mr. Rickaby's money still in her bag. "I haven't even a return ticket, and how I'm to get back I don't know."

"Don't worry about that," said Sir William. He paused, and Julia held her breath, because if he wanted an opening there was a beauty. But Sir William was still preoccupied with her extraordinary revelations.

"I'd like to know how you got here," he said, "if it won't make me an accessory after the fact."

"Oh, *no!*" cried Julia. "It was easy. I just sold some valuable furniture"; and since the moment for sentiment had obviously passed, she made a very good story out of Mr. Lewis and the bailiffs.

They had more weighty conversations, as well; for now that Julia knew Sir William better she was constantly on the lookout for an opportunity to talk about Susan and Bryan. Such an opening, however, was surprisingly difficult to find; Sir William had apparently cast all care aside, and refused to be drawn into any serious discussion. All he wanted was to lounge about the garden and listen to Julia's reminiscences, or else drive her about in the car and laugh at her appreciations of the scenery. "But it *is* a nice view!" said Julia once, indignantly. "Of course it is," agreed Sir William. "Then why do you laugh when I say so?" demanded Julia. "It's not what you say," explained Sir William, "it's your face while you say it. You have a special landscape-expression, my dear; you look so pleased with yourself. . . ."

Julia finally decided to count as an opportunity the first moment she could get Sir William alone when he wasn't actually laughing out loud. This occurred one fine, very hot morning, when they were both a little lazy in the heat, and when Anthelmine's visit was safely over. She had brought them a handful of *dragées,* the white sugared almonds that announced a wedding in the village; so the opportunity was really a good one.

"These are for Jeanne-Marie," said Julia. "Claudia's niece. She's getting married next week."

Sir William grunted.

"William!"

"What is it, my dear?"

"I want to talk to you seriously. About Sue and Bryan."

Sir William stretched himself in his deck-chair and looked at the sky. Julia understood his feelings; like any man happy and contented in the moment, he did not want to be bothered. Nor did she, for that matter; for no one else but Susan would she have disturbed, by so much as a thought, their delicious silent intimacy. But for Susan she had to do it.

"It's all my fault," she said cunningly.

At once, as she had known he would — and what happiness the knowledge gave her! — Sir William roused up.

"Nonsense, my dear! You've got an absolute passion for taking blame on yourself. How could it possibly be your fault?"

"Because I ought to have been firm as soon as I got here," said Julia seriously. "As soon as I *knew* — and while Susan was readier to hear what I said. I ought to have told her straight out that he was no good. I ought to have led him on and shown him up, even if it meant showing myself up too. But I left it, partly because I did so want her to think well of me, and partly because I knew she'd be so hurt. I haven't got a really hard heart."

"That's true enough," agreed Sir William.

"You see, I'm *sure,*" continued Julia earnestly. "It must seem odd to hear me say I understand a girl like Susan, but I do. She's very obstinate, and very proud. However badly Bryan turned out she'd never leave him or divorce him or — or do any of the other things. She'd just hang on, miserable, trying to keep up appearances. She'd take up welfare work, I expect, and eat her heart out."

"I should imagine welfare work would be rather Susan's line," said Sir William.

"Of course it is. She ought to be an M.P. — her grandmother thinks so too. But how can she put her heart into anything, when she's miserable at home?"

"Won't she be equally miserable if she's separated from Bryan now?"

"But only for a while," said Julia eagerly. "She'll get over it. She's only twenty. I know if she doesn't marry Bryan she won't marry anyone else for a long time, but I believe that's a good thing. Susan wants someone older than herself, someone with a position, who'll appreciate her. I can't quite explain it, but she needs ideas more than people. She's got ideas about herself. If you ask me, I believe Bryan's the first young man who ever had the nerve to make love to her, and she feels if she doesn't stick to him she'll be letting herself down. . . . You haven't gone to sleep again, have you?"

"No," said Sir William, "I'm considering. And I think you're right, my dear. Only what do you want me to do?"

"An awful lot," admitted Julia. "In the first place, I want you to give Bryan a bad time. Talk to him about settlements, and how you're going to tie up Susan's money, and ask when he's going to do a bit of work, and how soon you can see his father. He hates that kind of thing. If he can put it off by not being officially engaged for another year, he will. And then, for Susan — I want you to have her in town with you, and give dinner parties, and make her meet a whole lot of nice men."

Sir William considered this without enthusiasm.

"Susan's still at Cambridge," he objected. "She won't desert her French to help me entertain."

"But she gets a great long Christmas holiday," retorted Julia. "I'm not worrying about her while she's at college. A month or two back in her own atmosphere will do her good — and besides, if you begin too soon she'll smell a rat. Christmas is just the time."

"And I don't know any young men. I haven't for years."

"I didn't say young, I said nice. I know as well as you that Susan won't care for dancing. The sort you want are the serious ones — interested in the slums, and all that. If they ask her to serve on committees, she'll have the time of her life."

Sir William groaned.

"I've spent a lifetime on committees already — "

"There you are!"

"And I've had enough of them. I was going to write my last letter of resignation to-night."

"What from?" asked Julia quickly.

"A new sort of club affair in the East End. All very self-governing and educational. I had a letter from the secretary last night, asking if I'd mind submitting a provisional constitution, together with estimates for expenses and a draft appeal for public support."

"And you're not going to do it?"

"I'm going to send a cheque instead. From now on, *I*'m the public."

Julia jumped up, her face radiant.

"We won't have to wait after all," she said joyfully. "It's the very thing! Where's Susan?"


### 3

Susan was in the garden-room, filling her vases. For Sir William, who shared Julia's indifference to tangles, she had just completed a fine Dutch flower-piece of small early dahlias and red jasmine. She would have made a good florist, and knew it. Sometimes, in the abundance of her energy, she toyed with the idea of running a flower-shop as a sort of side-line to more important activities. She felt she could run any number of things — a career for Bryan, and one for herself, and probably her mother's cake-shop (if it ever materialized) into the bargain. At the moment, occupied by no more than French literature and a lover, she was feeling vaguely underexercised. It was therefore with extreme pleasure, as Julia had foreseen, that she listened to her guardian's proposal.

"But of course, Uncle William!" she cried. "I've done settlement work already, for school. I'd love to help, if you think I can be useful."

"I'm sure you'll be very useful indeed," said Sir William sincerely. Not one of that extremely well-meaning committee had Susan's energy — but then not one of them had Susan's youth. A pair of charitable dowagers, an M.P., an unpaid secretary, and — yes, that fierce, rather dishevelled young man who was the prime mover. *He* had energy enough — but no tact. If he and Susan ever got together, they would make, thought Sir William, a formidable team. . . .

"I ought to tell you," he said, "that there's prob-

ably another scheme being got out, by a fellow called
Bellamy. He'll probably tear everything you suggest
to pieces. He always does."

Susan opened her eyes.

"Bellamy! The Bellamy who wrote *Civics of the
Slums?*"

"Very likely," replied Sir William, with amazing
indifference. "I know he's written something. If
you'll come along, I'll give you all the stuff."

Half an hour later Susan was seated in the billiard-
room surrounded by a plan of the new premises, all
the information so reluctantly acquired by Sir William, and a mass of pamphlets on club management.
She was perfectly happy. As soon as Bryan came back
from the lodge, she intended that he should share her
joy.

# Chapter 18

A new and remarkable atmosphere now descended upon the villa. When Julia first arrived there she had been struck by its air of lazy peace; all that was now changed. Susan went about looking exactly like the secretary of a committee, always with a pamphlet in her hand or a bundle of foolscap under her arm. Nor did she stop at carrying the things about with her; among the papers turned over by Sir William were the plans of the proposed club; Susan traced them in triplicate (to work out alternative forms of cloak-room accommodation) and pinned them to the billiard-room wall. Whenever Julia looked up from a bridge-hand she saw the words "Lavatories" in red ink. All this businesslike activity, moreover, stimulated Mrs. Packett afresh, and she telegraphed home to an estate agent for particulars of vacant shops in the Kensington district. The agent, also stimulated, telegraphed back, at such length, and detailing such enormous rents, that the old lady, as well as everybody else at the villa, was quite appalled. "What did you say in *your* wire?" they asked; but Mrs. Packett would not tell them. Undaunted, she next entered into correspondence with a number of gentlefolk who were advertising in the *Lady* for "partners with capital." Some of them wired as well, saying "OFFER OPEN TWO DAYS ONLY," or "MANY APPLICANTS WILL YOU CLOSE AT ONCE?" By such innocent devices did they try to lure Julia into their tea-shops. Mrs. Packett, who was by now having the time of her life, wired back all round saying "NO SEND PARTICULARS AND BALANCE-SHEET" — and then the balance-sheets arrived, and she made Sir William check them.

"It's awful," admitted Julia gloomily; "but what can I do, William? I can't *tell* her. . . ."

"I suppose not," said Sir William, looking up from the highly complicated accounts of the Singing Samovar. "But it's rather hard on me. I might just as well be back in Whitehall."

"Couldn't you make Bryan do them?"

"He can't add. Anyway, he's being roped in to draw up articles of partnership."

Julia sighed. She hated the idea of yet another link between herself and that objectionable young man, but the fact remained that she and Bryan and Sir William had instinctively grouped themselves into a passively resisting minority. In numbers, it is true, they were superior, but Susan and her grandmother had the moral ascendency. They were Packetts. Julia resented their activities with all her heart, but she had never had a greater respect for her late husband's family.

"Here's Susan now," she said. "Give me one of those sheets to look at. . . ."

Susan, however, had not come in search of assistants; she merely wanted to know Mr. Bellamy's private address.

"Because I think I'd better write to him direct, Uncle William," she said; "then if there are any of my ideas he'd like to use, he can incorporate them with his own. It's no use putting two schemes in front of a committee; they simply start to argue."

Sir William looked at her with healthy mistrust.

"Wonderful," he said. "Have you been reading Bacon?"

Susan laughed.

"I'd certainly put a committee at a long table, and not a round one. One can't approve of him, but he did know how to get things done."

Sir William looked through his diary, found Mr. Bellamy's address, and wrote it down for Susan to take away. She went without lingering, brisk and businesslike; but both Julia and Sir William, instead of getting on with their work, sat gazing after her.

"She doesn't approve of Bacon," said Sir William at last. "If he were here, she'd certainly tell him so. And of course, she's perfectly right."

"She's always right," said Julia. It was wonderful to have a daughter who was always right, but even to her own ears, and as her next words betrayed, the tribute sounded cold. "She's a darling!" said Julia firmly.

Sir William went on with his accounts.

2

The third and youngest member of the minority, Bryan Relton, was having an even harder time than his elders. Like Julia, he had found in the original atmosphere of Les Sapins exactly the air that suited him, and the chill wind of efficiency, which now so steadily blew through it, did not brace him but simply made him shiver. Julia could at least warm herself in the comradeship of Sir William; Bryan was left out in the cold. When Susan first spoke to him of her new hobby he had been quite sympathetic and interested; if she liked that sort of thing, by all means (he felt) let her spend a wet afternoon making out plans. But the thing went on and on! Susan never forgot it! She was too strict with herself to neglect her studies, but the moment they were done she switched straight over to the Mile End Road.

"But it isn't the Mile End Road!" said Susan, in answer to one of her lover's complaints. "It's India Dock Lane." And she showed him the exact spot on a sketch-map. Bryan looked at it sulkily; to him the Mile End Road — or, for the matter of that, India Dock Lane — was less an actual locality than a frame of mind.

"If you're not interested," said Susan suddenly, "I wish you wouldn't pretend to be."

"Of course I'm interested, if you are."

"That's exactly what I mean. You're working up an interest just because of me."

"But that's being in love," pointed out Bryan. "Didn't you know?"

To his astonishment — for he rather expected a quarrel — Susan abruptly folded away the plan and asked him to come for a walk. They climbed the heights above Magnieu, up to the statue of the Virgin, and returned through woods. The views were magnificent, the conversation pleasantly light; but Bryan could not help feeling like a puppy being taken for a run.

### 3

With remarkable promptitude Mr. Bellamy replied; and Sir William, who happened to see the envelope, expressed his opinion to Julia that Susan was in for a bad quarter of an hour. For Mr. Bellamy had the habit of endorsing all suggestions which did not appeal to him with the one word "Rot!" He did it chiefly to relieve his feelings, and always meant to rub it out again if the papers were to be returned; but he was also absent-minded, and the habit had already lost him a philanthropic peer.

"He won't call Susan's scheme rot," said Julia indignantly, "because I'm sure it isn't." And as it happened she was right; Susan came out into the garden with a radiant face.

"I've had a compliment, Uncle William," she announced gaily. "Mr. Bellamy says I'm the first woman he's had to deal with who's got average common sense."

Julia looked at her daughter with wonder. If that was what Susan called a compliment . . . !

"You ought to be highly flattered," said Sir William. "I suppose that's the highest praise he's ever been known to give."

"It was the cloakroom arrangements for the girls," continued Susan. "I'd got in half as many lockers again, and no overcrowding. They're going to begin converting next month, Mr. Bellamy says, and if I'm in town he's asked me to go and see him."

"Then I'm only sorry you won't be," said Sir William "You might prevent his insulting the architect. We haven't had a libel action yet, but I expect one at any moment."

Susan gazed thoughtfully at the vineyard. Her longing was so evident that Julia marvelled again: from the expression on the child's face she might have been thinking about a hunt ball, or a new dance frock. It was really quite peculiar! But it was encouraging as well, and as soon as Susan had gone away — her visits were never long, because she had so much to do — Julia sat up with a pleased and maternal countenance.

"What's he like, William?"

"Who, my dear?"

"This Mr. Bellamy, of course. The one Susan's so struck on."

Sir William looked at her with appreciation.

"You've a wonderfully active mind, Julia. Have you been crying in the front pew already?"

"Certainly not," retorted Julia. "I've never cried at a wedding in my life." She paused, and with her usual honesty added, "Not that I've been to many. They don't seem to come my way." And at that she had to pause again, while a fine blush — the first for twenty years — overspread her face. For how dreadful if he should think . . . if she should seem to be suggesting!

"My dear — " began Sir William.

"About this Mr. Bellamy," said Julia hastily. "Tell me what he's like."

Sir William considerately did so.

"An untidy-looking beggar," he said. "Unmarried, about thirty. Too honest to be popular, but highly intelligent."

"Is he good-looking?"

"In a hungry sort of way I suppose he is. Rather like a Victorian curate gone Communist. I believe his father was an Oxford don."

Julia sighed, half regretfully, half with relief. Though the young man sounded pretty dreadful to her, he seemed also to have most of the qualities Susan approved. It was a pity he was so far away.

"I ought to warn you," added Sir William, "that as Susan's trustee I should be forced to disapprove. If he ever makes two hundred a year, that will be his limit."

Susan's mother smiled indulgently. She knew perfectly well that if both Susan and she were set on a thing, Sir William wouldn't have a chance.

### 4

Although, by comparison with her daughter and mother-in-law, Julia at this time appeared completely idle, such an impression was deceptive. She had one constant, unguessed-at occupation. She was being good.

She had often wanted to be good before. She had
a great admiration for goodness; she loved it sincerely
and humbly, as a peasant loves a saint. If she had
never been good before it was not because her spirit
was unwilling, but because her flesh was so remarkably weak. She needed help — all the help she could
get; and if help now came from a wholly personal
and emotional source, from the fact that she loved Sir
William, Julia was not proud enough to reject it.

Whether Sir William loved her in return she was
not yet sure; but he at least liked her, and she could
not bear that even his liking should have an unworthy
object. She now knew what had made her send back
Mr. Rickaby's money; it was the first instinctive step
in her new direction. Looking back on her behaviour
at Aix, Julia was seized by so severe a fit of remorse
that for some moments she believed it to be indigestion;
then she took comfort from the thought that only
genuine repentance could have produced such a strong
effect. If you repented, that was enough. You were
forgiven and could start again. Julia wished passionately that she were a Roman Catholic, so that she
could make one enormous confession — from the heart,
holding back nothing — and then be told she was all
right. She ought, she knew, to be able to believe that
by herself, out of pure faith; but she wanted telling.
They might make her do things in penance — wear

a hair-shirt, for instance: Julia would have welcomed one. She did give up sugar in her tea and coffee. And she carefully and conscientiously examined her wicked heart.

It wasn't, she decided tentatively, all bad. She could not remember being really unkind to anyone, or mean to another woman. She hadn't been a gold-digger. Her two great faults were not having remained at Barton, and — and the Mr. Macdermots. They were black. "But I've repented!" cried Julia to herself. "I'll never do anything like that again!" And she made a great, a soul-shaking resolution: that if nothing happened about Sir William, she would tell Mrs. Packett all, even how she had lost her money, and ask to be taken back to Barton for the rest of her virtuous life.

Julia did not regard this prospect exactly with gladness; but then she hadn't been good very long.

# Chapter 19

The next afternoon found Julia ridiculously unhappy because Sir William wouldn't be in to tea. He was driving Susan over to Belley to collect some books ordered through the local librarian, and the whole trip shouldn't have taken more than twenty minutes; but just as they were starting, and just as she, Julia, had refused to accompany them, Mrs. Packett most officiously suggested that they should stay and take tea out. This meant an absence of at least an hour, and Julia, too self-conscious to change her mind, had been suffering ever since from a sense of injury. It was idiotic, and she knew it; but to such an imbecile condition had love reduced her.

The conversation at the tea table did nothing to raise her spirits.

"Has Susan told you of her new idea?" asked Mrs. Packett. "She wants us to go back a week early."

"Why?" asked Bryan suspiciously.

"To watch them convert that club, of course," said Julia.

"Not only for that, my dear. She thinks it would be so nice," explained Mrs. Packett, "if we could all look for your shop together."

For a moment Julia was speechless. She would never have credited her daughter with so much duplicity. And yet — was it? Was it not rather just one more example of Susan's wonderful gift for tactful organization? She honestly believed, no doubt, that such a scheme would be acceptable all round; but to Julia, whose time lately had all been spent in managing Susan, it came as something of a shock to find Susan managing *her*.

"And I must say," continued Mrs. Packett, "that a week in town sounds very nice. We could go to the theatres, Julia dear; if Susan's too busy we could go by ourselves, in the evening. Susan always takes me to a matinee, in case I'm tired at night; but I'd lie down beforehand, after lunch."

"Of course we'll go!" cried Julia, suddenly touched. "And to a night club afterwards, if you like!"

The old lady looked wistful.

"I don't know about that, my dear. But we'll have dinner first, at one of the large hotels. Just a glass and a half of champagne each. . . ."

Bryan whistled.

"I think I'd better come too and keep an eye on you," he said. "It sounds to me as though you'll want bailing out."

Julia looked at him severely.

*"You'll* be with Susan," she said, "down in the East End. You'd better learn how to gargle." And before he could think of an answer — before she herself could become more deeply committed to Mrs. Packett's riotous plans — Julia got up and strolled towards the house.

It was the simple and devastating truth that no plan meant anything to her unless it involved Sir William. Until she knew what Sir William wanted her to do — until she knew what he was going to do himself — she was like a ship without a course, like a weather-cock waiting for a wind. If he wanted her to keep a cake-shop, she felt she could do even that. She could do anything! Anything in the world, if he would only tell her what! If he told her to go into a con-vent — "But they'd turn me out," thought Julia, with a sudden return to common sense. She sat down, just where she was, in the entrance hall, and tried to make that common sense work. Suppose, after all, he just wasn't interested? Suppose his own plans, already cut and dried, took no account of her what-ever? Might it not be that their happy, perfect intimacy, to her the most precious thing life could ever hold,

was to Sir William simply a pleasant holiday friend-
ship, and no rarer than any other? "Then I'm done
for," thought Julia. "I'll just have to grin and bear it."
She tried to grin then, and found it extraordinarily
difficult. She felt like a set of teeth in a dentist's window. The vigour of this image, and the fear that
someone might pass through the hall, brought her
to her feet; she didn't want to be found looking like
a sick Cheshire Cat.

"It'll all be the same in a hundred years," thought
Julia gloomily; and meanwhile wandered out again,
into the neglected part of the garden, where no one
ever went.

2

Four miles away in Belley, at a table outside the con-
fectioner's in the square, Susan and Sir William were
finishing their tea. They were both rather silent, but
whereas Susan was conscious of this, and wanted to
resume, or rather redirect, the conversation, Sir William was not. His eyes were fixed on the top storey
of a tall grey building immediately opposite — a top
storey which was unoccupied, slightly dilapidated like
the rest of the building, but which possessed a deep
triple-arched loggia. There was an odd charm about
the place — it was like a crow's nest over Belley, and

·in summer breakfast on that balcony, with the town stirring below, and a distant view of the hills, would be pleasant indeed. . . .

Sir William suddenly found himself thinking that he would like to live there with Julia.

This extraordinary notion both astonished and pleased him. He had not believed himself capable — for the last twenty years he hadn't been capable — of such a juvenile emotion. He was like a man who discovers that he can still touch his toes. And other, equally juvenile ideas came thronging after the first. He remembered a square in Cracow where all the houses were painted with bright designs, the square where they held the flower market. His eye had been caught there, in just the same way, by a little blue room, an afterthought of a room, perched like a cottage on top of a tall green-and-yellow building; now, after an interval of seven years, he mentally placed Julia at the window. And there were other places as well: Paris in springtime — "Good God!" thought Sir William. "Isn't that the title of a song?" — and the English countryside in June, and London in autumn when dusk came down like blue smoke. He knew what Julia would say to all of them — "Isn't that pretty, William?" or "I do like a nice view!" — yet for some reason the very ineptitude of her remarks only made her company more desirable. They were so funny. They made him feel at once amused and tender. . . .

"There's no doubt about it," thought Sir William, as though he had reached the end of an argument. Then his mind wandered off again, this time to the Riviera.

Susan meanwhile had eaten two chestnut-cakes, and now felt that the time had come for a little serious conversation. Serious conversation at the villa was always liable to interruption, either from her suitor or her mother, and while she had been quite genuine in her desire to visit the librarian, she was also glad of an opportunity to get Sir William to herself.

"You've never told me," said Susan abruptly, "what you think of Bryan."

Sir William detached his gaze from the balcony and came reluctantly back to earth.

"Does it matter?" he asked.

"Well," said Susan, somewhat taken aback, "I'd naturally like to know how you feel about him. I mean — isn't that what you came for?"

"So it is," said Sir William, with an air of surprise. "However, as you're determined to marry him in any case, there doesn't seem much point in a discussion. I believe I'll have another cup of tea."

Susan's eyes over the teapot, as she poured out for him, were both watchful and puzzled. She evidently suspected some trap; she simply could not believe in a genuine lack of interest.

"That sounds as though you didn't like him," she persisted. "Why?"

"I neither like nor dislike him," said Sir William. "He seems to me much the same as any other young man. He's got some money and a profession, we know who his people are; and as soon as you're twenty-one if you want to marry him you can. Now what about getting home?"

Susan obediently rose and accompanied him back to the car. Her countenance was placid, but she felt a vague dissatisfaction. Put into words — into such words as Julia used — it would have amounted simply to this: Sir William wasn't making enough fuss.

"If you've any real objection — " she began.

"I haven't," said Sir William swiftly.

"I'm perfectly willing to listen to you. Just as I've listened to Grandmother and to Julia. I'm not unreasonable."

"It is the height of unreason," pointed out Sir William, "to go on discussing a question after your mind is made up. It's a sheer waste of everyone's time."

Susan was silent. She had too clear a head not to see Sir William's point, but for once a logical position was not comfortable to her. Always, before, when she thought of her marriage, she had seen it on the other side of an obstacle — an obstacle of which the chief manifestation was precisely those discussions which Sir William had just put an end to; now she saw it quite close. There was no obstacle any more. With Sir William on her side, or at any rate not opposing her, she could marry Bryan Relton the moment she was twenty-one.

Susan remained silent.

### 3

High up on a terrace in the vine Bryan Relton lay on his back and looked at the clouds. Like Julia, he had left the tea table in a somewhat troubled frame of mind; but the pleasantness of his situation had already made him forget the worst of his cares. They had never been heavy: they were like the clouds — small, and as yet hardly approaching the sun. Susan's new preoccupation was one of them; he was getting very tired of her continual cloakrooms, and if she were going to make a habit of them . . .

He rolled over — the clouds seemed suddenly larger than he had thought — and reached for a stem of grass. It was not the best chewing sort, but the sensuous pleasure of drawing it from its sheath for a moment completely absorbed him. He put his face down close and snuffed deeply, like a young animal. Scent of dry soil, sweeter scent of clover! By raising his head he got a whiff of cool breeze: then down to the warm earth again, and the clover sweeter than before. It was the very epicureanism of the nose. His imagination began to range — to bonfires, to tar oozing on a ship's deck, to bacon cooking for breakfast, even to the hot petrol-laden air of Piccadilly on a summer afternoon. They were all good, and the world was full of them. There simply wasn't enough time to do them all justice — nor to see all the sights, and hear all the sounds, that clamoured for attention. Properly to appreciate everything, felt Bryan, was a full-time job; and he was forced to admit, as he meditated, that the late and great Victorian, Mr. Rudyard Kipling, had exactly formulated his creed. "For to admire and for to see" — it couldn't be better put. And there was the other chap, who wanted to stand and stare. . . . "Rum if I were to turn out a poet!" thought Bryan; but he knew himself too well to nourish false hopes. He wasn't creative. He'd never do any work in the world, but at least he'd be grateful.

It suddenly occurred to him that in this scheme of existence he had left out Susan. At the thought of her, and particularly at the thought of their walk back from Belley, his conscience stirred. He had promised — all sorts of things: diligence, sobriety, every human virtue. Impossible promises, which surely she had taken at their right emotional value! "She must know what I'm like!" argued Bryan. "She won't expect miracles!" He buried his face once more in the grass, drew in the fragrance, and wished she were there with him. He had an obscure conviction that if Susan could once feel the power of that warm earthy smell, he would be able to convert her.

He was back at the old place. He was still in pursuit.

"Blessed Susan!" said Bryan into the grass. The blades brushed against his lips, alive and springy; he had just time to enjoy the sensation before falling asleep.

## 4

It would have been sentimentally appropriate if Susan, on her return from Belley, had gone up and found him there and waked him with a kiss; but she went straight into the house to undo her books, and it was Julia, fleeing into the vine before the approach of the car, who unromantically tripped on his shins. Bryan sat up, rubbed himself, and at once perceived that he would get no sympathy.

"That's a silly place to lie!" said Julia. "Right in the path for people to fall over you!"

"If people looked where they were going," retorted Bryan, "other people wouldn't get trampled on. Is Susan back?"

"I expect so. I've just heard the car."

"And Sir William," murmured Bryan. "Now we shall both have company again."

Under his inquisitive eye Julia walked a little along the terrace and sat down on a large rock. She couldn't go back into the garden, and her roamings had tired her.

"I expect Susan's looking for you," she said.

"I've no doubt of it," agreed Bryan complacently. "I can also take a hint. Have you an assignation, darling?"

Julia did not deign to answer. Instead of departing, the young man strolled over and dropped down at her feet.

"It's wonderful," he said companionably, "what a knack we both have for attracting our betters."

"I don't know what you mean," said Julia.

"Don't be modest, darling. You know perfectly well Sir William's fallen for you."

In her heart, and despite her recent sad communings, Julia did know, and the thought gave her a secret delight; but she had no intention of sharing it with Bryan.

"You shouldn't talk like that about him," she said sharply. "You ought to have more respect."

Bryan grinned.

"So you've fallen for *him*, have you? What a place this is!"

"You're right there," agreed Julia seriously. "It's

all these views and rosebushes. I remember the first morning — when you made a fool of me — I was thinking the very same thing. And that's all it is with Sir William. He doesn't mean anything."

"But even his non-meanings are sacred? You'd better look out for yourself, darling."

Julia got up and walked to the edge of the terrace. She was a good liar, but she didn't want Bryan staring into her face. For — why not admit it? — it wasn't just the rosebushes. She could tell that. She could tell not by the way Sir William looked at her, but by the way he didn't look at her — at table, for instance, and when there were other people there. He didn't want them to see, and no wonder. . . .

"When you're Lady Waring — " said Bryan behind her.

Julia turned on him.

"Don't say such things!"

"Why not? Wouldn't you like to be Lady Waring?"

"No, I wouldn't."

"Why not?" asked Bryan again.

"Because it's not my line. If you want to know, because I'm not good enough for him — just as you're not good enough for Susan."

"You mean if he asked you, you'd refuse?"

"Yes. And you've no business to talk to me like this. *We*'ve no business to talk about him. But there you

are," said Julia harshly, "I'm the sort of woman anyone talks to about anything. I can't keep them off."

She walked quickly along the terrace to where the
path branched up and down. Contrary to her usual
habit, she began to mount. Down — along the line
of least resistance — were people, and for once Julia
wanted to be alone. The truth she had just spoken
was bitter in her mouth: for a moment she had seen,
as though from outside herself, the kind of woman
she was; and the image was hateful to her. "If only
I'd known!" thought Julia desperately. If only she'd
known that — that this was waiting for her, how different she would have been! It was too late now, and
she knew it; the life she had been living had got
under her skin, into her blood, had become a part
of her that she could never now eradicate. For it
was all rot about repentance, really: it was no more
use repenting over spilt milk than crying over it.
You could mop the milk up and squeeze it back into
the jug, but it wasn't the same. It was dirty.

A tangle of blackberries barred her path; Julia
pushed through, scratching her arms, and taking a
queer pleasure in the pain. She was higher now than
she had ever been, on a narrow ledge so closely grown
with saplings that even where the cliff, on her left,
dropped steeply down, she could not see out. It was
like a strait green corridor, roofed against the sun.

Every now and again an outcropping boulder jutted across the track, and on one of these Julia at last sat down. She had tired her body, but her mind worked pitilessly on, marshalling one after the other all the most discreditable incidents of her life. The times when she had got tight, and done things she was sorry for afterwards. The times when she had made herself cheap, hanging round bars in the hope of a dinner. . . .

"Oh God!" prayed Julia aloud. "Don't let him ever know!"

The tears ran down her cheeks; she wiped them away, clumsily, with the flat of her hand; and as she sat there weeping a most curious image, born perhaps from that other image of the spilt milk, arose in her mind. She saw herself as a cup of clear water, which she herself was somehow bearing through a crowd, and which she should have carried carefully, steadily, losing not a drop, so that when *he* asked for it the cup was still full and unpolluted. But instead of that she had let anyone drink who wished, sometimes because of what they gave her, mostly just because they were poor thirsty devils. . . .

"How could I tell?" demanded Julia of her Creator. "God, how could I tell?" Ah, but how could anyone tell? Suppose you carried your cup high, safe above those thirsty mouths, and at last there was no one to drink from it? Wasn't it better to have solaced a few poor devils by the way? And the strange image grew, till Julia saw all the race of women bearing their vessels of water and passing to and fro among the thirst-tormented race of men; and in the forefront she saw her daughter, carrying a cup of crystal, and holding it high above her head.

"I must be going mad," thought Julia, in real terror. She rose quickly; there was a wind among the treetops, soughing and whispering and shaking the leaves. The sound filled her with panic; she wanted to go back, yet the thought of the narrow leafy path was suddenly terrifying to her.

The air seemed darker. It wanted a full hour till sunset; but already she could apprehend the stealthy approach of night.

With quick, almost furtive steps Julia began to descend. So swiftly, so blindly had she come that the way back was now strange; twice she stood uncertain, and twice saw, or thought she saw, a movement in the trees behind. Her fear of the solitude changed to a fear of unknown company: the sensation of being watched, familiar even to those who walked habitually through woods alone, finally achieved her panic. She began to run, stumbling and hurting her feet on the up-thrust rocks. There were more of them than she remembered, and more blackberry-arms that caught at and tore her skirts. Julia wrenched herself free and ran on, faster and faster, till at last, unaware, she had passed the nut grove and the ruined pavilion. She had not realized her safety when a tall figure seemed to rise up in her path; with a cry of sheer terror she fell forward and was caught in Sir William's arms.

"I thought you were a ghost," sobbed Julia. The feel of his coat under her cheek was such a blessed reassurance that she clung closer still, till she rasped her skin on the rough tweed. For a moment Sir William said nothing, nor was speech needed. The firm clasp of his arm, like a strong barrier against the powers of darkness, was enough. Julia made herself small within it, blessing him from her heart.

"Did anything frighten you?" he said at last.

"No," sobbed Julia. "It was nothing. Only — I'm such a fool — I stayed up there too long, and I got scared. I don't know why."

"It's untilled ground," said Sir William quite calmly, as though that explained everything. "Come down to the house, my dear, and get warm."

But he did not move, nor did Julia. She just tilted back her head to receive his kiss.

5

"I've been wanting to do that for a long time," said Sir William.

"Then why didn't you?" asked Julia, with real curiosity.

They had walked a little way down the path, not far, but just into the open away from the trees. The rosebushes bounding the upper terrace still screened them from the house.

"Because I haven't been in love for a long time," said Sir William, "and it makes a man nervous."

Julia laughed, partly from pure happiness, partly from astonishment. That anyone could be nervous because of her was something so strange, as well as so delicious, that she could hardly credit it. Her eyes widened even as she laughed; she held Sir William by the coat and made him repeat the astounding, the rapture-inducing statement.

"But why, William? How could you be?"

"In case I spoilt everything. In case you refused me."

Julia stood very still. Refuse him? Didn't he know she couldn't refuse him anything? Or was he — was it possible?

It was possible. It was a miracle, but it happened. A moment later, in the plainest of terms, Sir William had asked her to marry him.

"No!" cried Julia, almost wildly. "No, of course not! I never heard of such a thing!"

And breaking from his arm she fled down the bank and ran for the shelter of the house.

# Chapter 20

Following the best Victorian precedent, Julia pleaded a headache, refused to come down to dinner, and drank a small bowl of soup in her room. Thither both Susan and Mrs. Packett, full of solicitude, came to visit her. "If they only knew!" thought Julia, obediently swallowing aspirins; but not a suspicion, it was plain, had crossed their minds. They talked of, and blamed, the thundery weather; they advised a quiet evening, or rather a long night in bed. Julia agreed to everything, and as soon as they were gone, dissolved — again following precedent — into a flood of nervous tears. The outburst relieved her; she washed her face, and sat down by the window, and tried to consolidate her moral position.

She had refused Sir William. For a while that one fact, so enormous, blocked out everything else. She had refused Sir William; and though her doing so had been, at the time, a simple involuntary reaction, she did not now, nor ever would, question the rightness of that decision. During her talk with Bryan and

her vigil on the hillside she had done all the thinking
necessary; her mind was firmly made up. Sir William,
in his blessed ignorance and uprightness, had asked
her to marry him; only by refusing could she, Julia,
reach up to his level.

"God knows how I did it," she thought, bowing
her head down on the window sill. "It must have
been because I hadn't time to think. . . ."

But she knew, with melancholy pride, that even if
she had thought it would have been the same. For
she would have thought of Susan. To marry Sir William would be to destroy the last argument against
Susan's marriage with Bryan; no use talking to Bryan
of incompatibility, if her own action, meanwhile,
spoke louder than any words! That afternoon, for
the first time, she had been conscious of making an
impression on him; how much stronger it would be
when he knew what she had done! For know he must,
even though it meant asking permission of Sir William first — and that would be almost the hardest
thing yet.

"If only I could get away!" thought Julia desperately. "If only I could cut it clean out!" The thought
of the morning, bringing its renewal of their intercourse, was terrible to contemplate; she could only
pray that Sir William, like herself, would be willing
to wipe out and forget everything that had happened

since the moment when she so literally fell into his arms. Not that *she* would forget — ever; she would warm all her life with the beautiful memory; but she would behave as though she had. Gradually, firmly, she would withdraw from intimacy; become gently reserved; so that when at last they parted it would be merely as friends.

"If the truth were known," said Julia aloud, "I bet he's thanking his stars already."

Then she put her hand over her heart and pressed hard; because it really felt queer, like something heavy and bruised inside her. Renunciation scenes were all right on the stage; but in real life — and without an audience — there wasn't much fun in them. Julia got up and automatically began to tidy her hair; the face in the glass surprised her by looking very much as usual. "It's too round," thought Julia dispassionately. "I'm not built for tragedy" — and she was still scrutinizing herself when Susan tapped at the door and came quietly in.

"How are you now?" she asked. "I thought you might have gone to bed."

2

"No," said Julia, with a guilty start. "No, I haven't. I believe it's cooler."

"It is," agreed Susan. "There's almost a breeze. Uncle William thinks it might do you good if he took you for a short run in the car."

Julia started again. This was a frontal attack such as she had not contemplated, and such as she must at all costs repel.

"Thank him very much," she said quickly, "but I don't think I will. I believe I'd better stay quiet. I believe I'm going to bed."

Susan smiled encouragingly, like the best type of nurse.

"If you *can* make the effort, you know, I believe you'd feel better." Her eyes glanced over the soup bowl, which Julia, in spite of mental distress, had cleaned up with a piece of bread. "You get so much more air in a car."

"It's closed," said Julia, rashly entering into argument.

"But you can have all the windows open, and the roof. You can sit in the back by yourself and be perfectly quiet." Susan smiled again; her bedside manner was so perfect that Julia could almost smell the ether. She changed her line of defence.

"If you want to know, Sue, I don't like to give Sir William the trouble — "

"Then *that*'s all right," said Susan triumphantly, "because he's getting the car out now."

Five minutes later Julia found herself being tenderly delivered to her abductor at the foot of the porch steps. The car was as open as its Daimler nature permitted, there were rugs in case the night turned chilly, and a paper fan (supplied by Anthelmine) in case it perversely turned hot.

"Back or front?" asked Susan, as Bryan leapt gallantly forward to open the door.

Sir William looked round, full into Julia's face. "Back," said Julia.

With languid dignity she took her seat. As Bryan folded the rug over her knees, as the others stood watching from the steps, she began to feel as though she were really leaving a nursing-home for her first outing. It was a good moment in its way — and it was just like Bryan to go and spoil it.

"Bet you don't come home like that!" said Bryan cheerfully.

### 3

For perhaps three minutes the car and its two occupants slid silently through the dark. There was a breeze, as Susan had promised; but even physically Julia could not relax. She sat rigid in every limb, one hand clutching the rug, the other pressed hard against the seat. Totally incapable of speech herself, she equally feared and longed for Sir William's first words. When at last, from a slight movement of his head, she knew that they were coming, she could hardly draw breath.

"You must be damned hungry," said Sir William over his shoulder.

"I'm not!" gasped Julia.

"If you'd only told me," continued Sir William, unheeding, "I could have had a headache myself."

"I did have a headache!" cried Julia indignantly.

"Whether you had or you hadn't, I can quite believe you've got one now. The first thing we must do is to get you some food. Why are you sitting there in the back?"

"So that I don't have to talk," explained Julia, with as much sarcasm as she could muster. For some minutes she flattered herself that it had taken effect; but Sir William's next question was not reassuring.

"What was that young Relton said to you?"

"Nothing," snapped Julia. "At least — he said he was sorry for me being dragged out, just to please Susan, when I'd got such a headache."

"You'll be better when you've had some food," said Sir William.

Julia was now too exasperated to speak; but she was no longer tense. She threw herself back against the cushions with an audible thump; her brain worked naturally and furiously as she thought of more things to say to Sir William. Their skirmish had at least broken the ice, and as this thought crossed her mind Julia suddenly began to laugh.

"William!"

"My dear?"

"Did you do it on purpose?"

"Do what?"

"Make me lose my temper."

"Of course," said Sir William. "Now are you coming in front?"

He stopped the car; Julia bundled out and got in beside him. His object having been achieved, however, Sir William relapsed into silence; and indeed it was only a few minutes before the outskirts of Belley began to loom before them. They drew up not at the Pernollet, but, by Julia's choice, at a small café near the promenade. She selected it because there were plenty of people there, and because for once in her life she wanted chaperoning; she had not allowed for Sir William's English habit of lumping all foreigners with their natural and inanimate surroundings.

"Now then!" he said, as soon as Julia was supplied with an omelette and red wine. "It's customary, when refusing an offer of marriage, to give some reason. Even if you simply dislike the man, you're supposed to trump up some polite excuse as a salve to masculine pride."

"Dislike!" cried Julia, at once falling into the trap. "If you think that, you — you can't have any sense at all. I like you better than any man I've ever met."

"Thank you," said Sir William. "That's very handsome. Then why won't you marry me?"

Julia decided to tell a certain amount of the truth.

"Because it wouldn't be suitable. Because I wouldn't be the kind of wife people expect for you."

"Damn what people expect," said Sir William vigorously. "I've been doing what people expect all my life, and now I'm old enough to please myself."

Julia took a deep breath.

"You don't know anything about me — "

"I know quite enough. I know you make me enjoy things as I never thought I would again. I know that I have a most ridiculous desire, Julia, — since you're so obviously capable of looking after yourself, — to take care of you. You'll probably find me a thorough nuisance."

"Oh no, I shouldn't," said Julia earnestly. "I should simply love it. I've often looked at women with husbands — the nice sort, you know, who buy railway tickets for them — and thought how lovely it must be." She paused, aware that this was not the line she had intended to take, and began again. "There are things I ought to tell you — "

"Don't," said Sir William. "I haven't been a hermit

myself, but I'm not going to bore you with the details."

"I shouldn't be bored a bit," said Julia, who had no tact.

"In any case I shan't tell you. We start clear from now."

"But I *must* tell," said Julia desperately. "You see, if, when we both left here, you'd asked me to go to Aix with you — or anywhere else, for that matter — I'd have come like a shot. Just for a week, or as long as you wanted me. I — I'd come now."

"I know you would, my dear."

"Well?" said Julia, staring straight in front of her.

"I don't want you just for a week," explained Sir William. "I want you for always. And I'm too old, my dear, to go about staying in hotels under assumed names. I should find it a great nuisance."

"We could take a villa somewhere," suggested Julia seriously.

"That would be even more conspicuous," said Sir William.

Involuntarily Julia sighed. She was loving him more and more all the time, and it didn't make things easier. But she thought of Susan and hardened her heart.

"There's something else, William — no, not about me; about Sue and Bryan. I've told him again and again that people as different as they are haven't a hope. But we're just as different ourselves: you're good, like Susan, and I'm the same sort as he is — and what's more, he knows it. If I go and marry you, he'll just think it's all rot."

"So it is," said Sir William.

"About us, perhaps," admitted Julia. "But then you're different again. You're not *pure* good, like Sue. You're older, and you've knocked about a bit, and you wouldn't expect so much. But Bryan won't see all that; he'll just see that I've practised one thing and preached another, and he'll never believe a word I say again. You know what the young are."

"I know one thing," said Sir William, "and that is that I strongly object to being made the sacrifice."

"He'd want a double wedding," prophesied Julia, still following her own train of thought; "it's just what he'd enjoy. He'd go and marry Susan just to see my face. I'm sorry, William dear."

Sir William was apparently following his own train of thought too.

"I can understand that you're afraid of getting tired of me — "

"No!" cried Julia, stung. "Never! You mustn't think that of me, William! I know — I could swear — that if I married you I'd never look at another man so long as I lived. I wouldn't want to. I've got an awful lot of — of faithfulness in me, if you can only believe it. . . ."

"If I didn't believe it," said Sir William gently, "I shouldn't have asked you to marry me. But I think it's only for the one right man, my dear, and if I'm not he — "

"But you are!" wailed Julia, almost in tears. "I've known it all along, and that's what's so awful. You can't think how I want to — to show you. I've sometimes wished — no, not wished, just imagined — that you were a hopeless invalid, or paralyzed, or something, so that I could just be there looking after you for years and years. I'd love it!"

For a moment Sir William did not speak; and indeed so forcible an expression of devotion was enough to silence any man. Then he reached out and put Julia's coat round her shoulders.

"Come back to the car," he said.

"No," said Julia wretchedly. "Once you start kissing me, I'll be done."

"We've got to get back some time," pointed out Sir William.

"Not till I've made you understand." Julia sat up, and as a sign that she had fully recovered herself even managed to smile. "You've made me prouder than I've ever been in my life, William, only it's no use.

There's too much against it. I can't say all I feel, I never could; but you'll always be a beautiful memory."

"Julia!" said Sir William sharply.

"What, darling?"

"You're enjoying yourself."

Julia flushed. It was only too true that in spite of her real misery, she had been conscious of speaking that last line well.

"And what's more," continued Sir William, "you're enjoying yourself at my expense. I should simply loathe to be a beautiful memory. As you can't talk sense, you'd better come home."

This time Julia rose. There was no doubt about it, Sir William possessed an extraordinary knack of tipping up the highest moral plane. Slightly ruffled by her sudden descent, Julia powdered her nose with vigour and in silence, and accompanied him back to the car.

But at least she was right about one thing. As soon as he began kissing her, she was done.

4

"Shall I have to open bazaars?" asked Julia about an hour later.

They were driving slowly up from the Lac du Bar. Their homeward route had been by no means direct.

"Good heavens, no!" said Sir William.

Julia was reassured, but also a little disappointed. She could just fancy herself on a platform, in very good black, with a spray of orchids at the left shoulder. . . .

"You won't have any of that," continued Sir William, "and we can live wherever you like. At the moment I've a flat in Town — "

"Where?" asked Julia.

"Mount Street. You may like it. And of course if we keep that on, instead of taking a house, we can go abroad whenever we want to. I'd like to take you abroad, Julia. You enjoy things so."

Julia rubbed her cheek against his coat. She couldn't kiss him, because he was driving.

"I'd like to go to Venice. Louise — a girl I used to know once — went there, and she said it was heavenly. . . . William!"

"Well?"

"When I talk about people like that — people who may be a bit rum — does it worry you?"

Sir William put down his left hand and felt for hers.

"Not in the least, my dear. You have the most entertaining friends of anyone I've met."

"That's lucky," sighed Julia; "because I expect I shall a good bit. And Louise was an awfully good sort. . . . If you're going to stop the car, darling, do it before the village."

Ten minutes later, at the villa gates, she asked him to stop it again — this time merely to let her get into the back.

"Thank you," said Sir William. "I must admit I've been curious."

"Curious?" repeated Julia in surprise. "Why, what have I told you?"

"What young Relton said as we started," replied Sir William. "And he ought to be kicked for it."

# Chapter 21

The last action of Julia's free will, before she finally and joyfully submerged it in Sir William's, was to persuade him not to announce their engagement. Sir William wanted to do things at once, thoroughly, and get them over; he wanted to send a notice to the *Times,* tell the Packetts, and marry Julia as soon as possible. Flattering as this programme was, and much as Julia longed for its completion, she nevertheless held him back. She feared the consequences —and not only upon Bryan: she had an uneasy conviction that the Packetts wouldn't believe it. They would just think that Sir William had gone mad, and that she was abetting him. Rather to her surprise, Sir William, when she laid this view before him, was very much annoyed.

"My dear Julia," he said firmly, "if that's your only objection I shall go straight into the billiard-room and tell them now. There's no other way of showing you how foolish you are."

Julia jumped up — they were sitting in their usual place among the vines — and seized his arm.

"Don't, William! Not just yet! I'm a fool all right — I'm anything you say — but it isn't *that* only. I've got to think of Susan and Bryan. I've got to get that business settled first."

"It's settling itself," retorted Sir William. "It's settling itself perfectly. Young Relton is at last finding out what Susan's really like, and Susan — who must have found him out long ago — is beginning to realize that she'll never change him. In a couple of weeks, and especially if Susan goes to London, the whole thing will have blown over."

Julia tightened her grip.

"Then don't you see how important it is that they shouldn't be — be disturbed? It's not only that club business, William, — and that was my idea too, — it's partly what I've been saying to Bryan. I *have* influenced him, though he wouldn't admit it. And now if we go and get married he'll forget everything else and send their engagement to the *Times* as well, and quite likely go back to London himself and start working like hell and all — " Julia gasped for breath — "out of cussedness. We must leave things alone, William. You say yourself it's only a matter of weeks."

"And if it's longer?" enquired Sir William. "If it's two months, or two years? Are we to spend the rest of our lives waiting for two young idiots to come to their senses?"

"Now you're just being silly," said Julia comfortably. "And they're not idiots at all. They're just very young. I expect when *you* were young—"

"Thanks," said Sir William. "One of the things I like about you, my dear, is that you don't flatter me."

Julia slipped down onto the grass beside his chair and gave him one of her long, candid looks.

"I don't want you young, darling. I want you just as you are, experienced, and understanding, and—and able to deal with me. And besides—"

She broke off, still gazing, on a sigh of pure happiness. Sir William reached down and touched her cheek.

"Besides what, my dear?"

"You *do* look so distinguished!" said Julia simply.

An absurd glow of happiness took Sir William by surprise. There were many good reasons, he could not help knowing, why a woman in Julia's position should be glad to marry him, and in his more sober moments—when the fact that she had simply fallen in love with him seemed to pass belief—he had often enumerated them. But he had never yet included his personal appearance. . . .

"I see I was wrong," he said lightly. "You're a flatterer after all.

"I'm not flattering you a bit," said Julia earnestly. "I don't say you're the handsomest — I wouldn't say you were like poor Valentino — but you're the most distinguished-looking man, William, I've ever seen. It's your side-face, and your height, and the way you hold yourself. I thought it the moment I saw you."

"Then you must be in love with me," said Sir William.

As they went down to the house — the question of announcing their engagement tacitly shelved — he suddenly began to laugh. Julia asked why, but he would not tell her. She had explained so firmly that he was no longer young: and he had just caught himself wishing that instead of putting on a dinner-jacket, he could appear before her in his tail-coat.

2

There was no end, Julia felt, to the good things which were now being showered upon her. As though Sir William, and all he implied, were not enough, she received that evening the first real mark of Susan's affectionate confidence. Susan came in while Julia was changing for dinner and sat down — just like a daughter — on the edge of the bed.

"Uncle William's just told me," said Susan, "that

it was your idea about letting me in on this new club. What made you think of it?"

Julia smiled complacently.

"I knew it would be just the thing for you, Sue. I mean — I knew *you*'d be just the thing for them. You're so efficient, and clear-headed."

This answer, besides being for the most part true, was evidently the one Susan wanted. She looked at her mother with genuine warmth.

"You can't think how I like you to say that. The others — Bryan, and even Uncle William — seem to look on it simply as a nice hobby for *me;* they don't see the other point of view at all — that I'm possibly being of real use. You've got the right attitude."

"This is my lucky day," thought Julia; and determined to venture further.

"This Mr. Bellamy, Sue — when I'm back in Town, I think I'd like to meet him. Will it be all right if I just go down to the club?"

"Oh!" cried Susan, quite radiant at the prospect of at last making a convert. "Of course it will! I'll write and say you're coming. Only — are you quite sure it would interest you?"

Julia was certain. She had never met a man yet in whom she could not become interested at a moment's notice. It was Susan's interest she felt needed arousing — Susan's interest in Mr. Bellamy, not merely as a good worker, but as an individual young man.

"I hope he won't knock himself up," said Julia thoughtfully.

"Who? Mr. Bellamy?"

"Sir William says he isn't strong," explained Julia. "He says he's terribly thin. I expect he doesn't feed himself properly."

Susan looked serious.

"I hope he doesn't go sick, because he's really running the whole thing. He's really important. Listen, Mother — "

Julia's heart leapt. It was all she could do not to kiss Susan then and there, out of sheer gratitude. But she restrained herself. She knew that if Susan were once made self-conscious, that beautiful word would never be heard again.

"What is it, Sue?"

"I've been thinking — if I meet him in London, he'll probably want to stand me a meal, and I know he's awfully hard up. But if *you* asked us both to your flat — or I could ask him there myself, quite easily — "

"Of course!" cried Julia. "Of course you'll come! I'll give him roast beef and a suety pudding!"

At that Susan laughed, and Julia laughed too. She hadn't got a flat — she hadn't even a dining-table — and when she reacquired these things, by marriage with Sir William, Susan would quite likely disapprove and refuse to make use of them; but in spite of these obstacles Julia already saw, in her mind's eye, Susan and Mr. Bellamy sitting one on each side of her, exchanging looks of love above a well-spread board. The picture was so clear, and filled her with such confidence, that she ventured on a leading question.

"What about Bryan, Sue? Would he like to come as well?"

"Oh!" said Susan. For a moment it seemed as though she were really going to open her heart, and Julia, at the dressing-table, held her comb suspended. Then through the mirror she saw Susan slowly get up, smooth the counterpane where she had been sitting, and walk towards the door.

"No," said Susan casually, "I don't think Bryan would be interested. By the way, dinner's going to be a little early, because Anthelmine has the evening off."

Julia finished her dressing in great satisfaction. For the first time she felt herself to be completely accepted, by Susan, as Susan's ally. It was fortunate, since she enjoyed the sensation so much, that she could not see twenty-four hours ahead.

3

Twenty-four hours later an event took place in the village which had the extraordinary effect, at the villa, of ranging Julia on Bryan's side against her daughter.

Jeanne-Marie, the niece of Claudia, the distributor of sugared almonds, got married; and at the ensuing celebrations, Bryan got tight.

He went to the party alone, and, as afterwards transpired, was the life and soul of it. There was dancing, and he danced. There was singing, and he sang. (For several days afterwards Sir William, whenever he walked through the village, was constantly being surprised by the strains of "Forty Years On.") To support his energies he naturally needed a good deal to drink, and by the time the party broke up, shortly after midnight, it was obvious that he had had it. Even then all might have been well, for there were plenty of volunteers to escort him back to the lodge; but with the perversity of his condition he insisted on going up to the villa to bid his friends there good night.

By chance, and because of the heat, they were still in the billiard-room. Bryan flung open the door, skidded a little over the parquet, and came to rest on the chair next to Susan's. There he began to sing.

He was not drunk, but he was undeniably intoxicated.

At once Susan, Julia, and Sir William all rose from their seats; but whereas Susan instinctively backed away, her face white with anger, Julia and Sir William as instinctively approached.

"Stop it!" said Julia severely.

Bryan looked at her, his mouth still open on a high note, with natural surprise. People had applauded his singing all evening, why should they suddenly stop now?

"Why, darling?" he asked. "Tell me why?"

"Because you're disturbing Mrs. Packett," said Julia. She glanced over her shoulder, and was briefly struck by the calmness of that lady's demeanour. Mrs. Packett didn't look disturbed at all. Bryan meanwhile had risen to his feet, not from any personal volition, but because of Sir William's firm hand under his arm.

"I wouldn't like to do *that*," he said. "Wouldn't like to 'sturb anyone. Sue, darling — "

Susan walked straight past him and out of the room. He made a spasmodic effort to follow, and felt the restraining weight of Sir William.

"No, you don't," said Sir William. "Sue doesn't want disturbing either. You'd better come to bed."

"All right," agreed Bryan. "I — I'll jus' say good night. Good night, all!"

His innocuousness, in the face of Susan's demonstration, was almost pathetic. Sir William led him away, and all was still.

"Aspirin, I *think*," said Mrs. Packett. "There's some in my room."

"I've got some too," said Julia; and for once kissed her mother-in-law good night.

## 4

The following morning was an uneasy one. Bryan appeared about twelve o'clock, looking slightly pale, and apologized all round. By Mrs. Packett, Julia, and Sir William his expressions of regret were at once accepted; and they might all have been comfortable again but for the attitude of Susan. She too accepted his apology; but she could not forgive him. She did not — felt Julia — *want* to forgive; what he had done was in her eyes unpardonable, and the fact that her elders actually had pardoned it simply lowered her opinion of them as well. Julia saw this, and on Sir William's behalf was extremely annoyed; her heart was also touched by Bryan's mournful looks. Logically she should have rejoiced, but then logic was never Julia's strong point. She had made up her mind, however, not to interfere, and would probably have managed to hold aloof had not Susan deliberately brought up the subject in the garden after lunch.

"Grandmother has just been telling me," she said, with a lift of the eyebrows, "that *her* father was a three-bottle man. I suppose I'm to make a comparison."

"Your grandmother," said Julia sharply, "has more sense than anyone I know."

"Then you probably agree with her," said Susan, "that last night doesn't matter in the least?"

"Of course it doesn't!" cried Julia, roused from her neutrality. "Every young man gets a bit squiffy now and again — and that's when you see what they're like. Bryan — "

"Well?"

"He was sweet," said Julia firmly. "He didn't give a bit of trouble, and he isn't being proud of himself afterwards. You're behaving as though he got rolling drunk and chased the cook."

She broke off — a little alarmed, for her own sake, by the vigour of her language. It wasn't the sort of thing she ought to have said: it implied too much experience. But Susan did not appear to notice. She was withdrawn into her cloud.

"You think, then, that I'm uncharitable?" she said at last.

"No," said Julia slowly. She also had had time to reflect. "Only . . . you don't *like* people." She thought again, and changed the intonation. "You don't like *people*. You only like — it's so hard to explain — their good qualities."

"You don't expect me to like their bad?" asked Susan grimly.

"No," repeated Julia; "but if you liked *people,* their bad qualities wouldn't worry you so much."

Susan locked her hands in her lap and stared at the treetops. Her young figure was stiff with pride.

"I think you're wrong," she said. "I'm sorry. But then I don't think I need people so much as you do."

Julia could only hope that she was right; but an instinctive fear as to the results of such an outlook drove her on.

"At any rate, I think you ought to make it up with Bryan. If you must quarrel with him — "

"I've no intention of quarrelling with him," said Susan quickly. "I can't tell him it doesn't matter, but — but I'll be nice."

And that afternoon she was nice — so charming, so light-hearted, that Bryan was quite taken by surprise when she suddenly asked for his promise not to drink wine again so long as they were in France.

"But I'll look such a fool!" he said. "It's always on the table!"

"I'll drink barley-water too," promised Susan.

"No," said Bryan firmly. Susan's niceness had rather gone to his head: he felt that for the first time her rigid will showed signs of becoming more pliant. "No, darling; it's absurd. . . ."

Even then Susan only smiled. She remained charming to him all day. But on the dining-table that night he noticed, and everyone else noticed, that the carafe of *vin ordinaire* was only half-full.

# Chapter 22

In Julia's opinion it was that half-full carafe which led Bryan to view more seriously Susan's philanthropic activities. His subconscious was thoroughly alarmed, but at the same time refused to admit what had really frightened it. Julia knew a lot about the subconscious from Louise, who had once been psychoanalyzed with very exhilarating results. It therefore came as no surprise to her when Bryan cornered her alone in the billiard-room and observed that he was getting very tired of all this rot about clubs.

"It isn't rot," said Julia tartly. "It's a very good work."

"All right, darling. But I know Sir William ducked out of it."

"He needs a rest. He's on holiday."

"So is Susan. So — more to the point — am I. It was bad enough when she was always dashing off to read French, but this thing's the limit. She can't talk about anything else."

"Well, you'd better get used to it," said Julia calmly,

"because it's the sort of thing she'll be doing all her life. I expect you will too."

"Not me," said Bryan, in genuine alarm. "I've got too much sense. I know my own limitations. All I want is a quiet life. When you open your cake-shop, darling, I shall apply for a job as errand-boy."

"I'm not going to open a cake-shop," snapped Julia, whom this subject was beginning to infuriate.

"Not even for the sake of giving me employ? What do you expect to become of me?"

Julia considered.

"I shouldn't be surprised," she said thoughtfully, "if you were to turn out a journalist."

"That's clever of you, darling, because I've had the same notion myself. I'd make a damn good special cor-respondent. How did you tumble to it?"

"I used to know a lot," said Julia vaguely. "They never seemed to settle down. But what are you talking like this for? You're going to be a barrister!"

"Weather permitting, my dear. I'm not sure I should ever stick it. Besides, most barristers *are* journalists. That's how they earn the odd guineas to buy their beer."

Julia sat up in exasperation. "Can't you see," she wanted to say, "can't you *see* how hopeless it is?" But instead — for she was at last learning wisdom — she merely remarked that even if his own income proved insufficient, Susan's should at any rate be able to supply him with drinks.

"If you think I'm going to sponge on Susan —" began Bryan hotly.

"She'll have much more money than you will," Julia pointed out; "especially if you're going to be an errand-boy. I don't know exactly, but she'll have all the Packetts'."

Bryan stood up and walked quickly to the window.

"She'll probably give it all away," he said over his shoulder. "To these good works you're so keen on."

Julia nodded.

"Very likely. I expect she'll go in for them really seriously."

His fingers began to drum an impatient and angry tattoo.

"If you ask me," he said at last, "if you ask me —"

"I'm not asking, I'm telling you," said Julia. "It's what I've been telling you all along."

The next moment the door slammed behind him.

2

The party at luncheon was reduced by one: Mr. Relton had gone off on a long walk — so ran the message left with Claudia — and would not be back to tea. Julia looked quickly at her daughter, to see

whether the interview which she so confidently an-
ticipated had already taken place; judging by Susan's
countenance, it had not. Susan was openly annoyed,
because she had desired Bryan's company for a trip
to Belley, and her afternoon's plans were thus dis-
arranged; but she showed no sign of having been faced
with the disarrangement of her whole future. Her
future, as it happened, was what she chiefly talked
about, and it was concerned so largely with the prob-
lems of club management that Julia could not help
wondering whether the absence of Bryan would really
disarrange it all. "She'll get over it sooner than I
thought!" Julia told herself happily. "If only she can
keep her opinion of herself, she'll be right as rain!"
A wound to Susan's self-esteem was the only one Julia
really feared, and if the break came from Bryan — as
it would — even that might be avoided: Susan wouldn't
have let him down; she would have kept, scrupulously,
her side of their mutual promise. For Bryan's self-
esteem Julia didn't care a rap, and so she told Sir William when she met him, at three o'clock, in the ruined
pavilion.

They met there every afternoon, stealing up — at
least Sir William walked, but Julia definitely stole —
from the quiet house while its other inhabitants took
their siestas. There was no actual reason, of course, why
they should not have ascended boldly side by side, but

Julia's romantic and sentimental heart — had she not
drawn it, in lipstick, on the pavilion wall? — always
missed a beat as she pushed through the nut trees and
found Sir William waiting for her. She enjoyed that
moment too much to forgo it, even though they never
stayed longer than five minutes, because there was
nowhere to sit. . . .

"As for Bryan, I don't care a rap," said Julia. "He
ought to be just plain grateful to me." As always on
leaving the pavilion, she put out her hand and with
a light caressing gesture touched the lipstick heart.
Sir William turned back from the steps to watch her.
"And if he isn't now," continued Julia, her rite performed, "he will be in a week or two. I've been an
absolute providence to him."

"If not a mother," agreed Sir William. "Would you
like to go over and dine at Aix?"

"In evening dress?" asked Julia at once.

"Certainly," said Sir William. "That's mainly why
we're going. I have a craving to put on tails."

"I bet you look a dream in them," said Julia sincerely.
She let him help her down to the path, and there stood
a moment in thought. But she was no longer thinking about Bryan. "I can't do much myself," she said
regretfully, "because my wardrobe's a bit low. I've got
a lovely dark-blue taffeta, only I don't know if you'll
like the top. I mean, there practically isn't any — not

even shoulder straps. I don't mean it isn't *decent,* because it is; but it's a bit — well, dashing. I've got a nice lace scarf, though; it used to be white."

"And what colour is it now?" asked Sir William with interest.

"Écru. I lent it to Louise once, and she got into a roughhouse somewhere — just like she always did — and upset coffee right across the middle. So we made a lot more, in a hand-basin, and dipped the whole thing, and it came up beautifully. And then Louise went and spilt the whole basinful, right down her frock!"

"It's like the House that Jack built," observed Sir William, fascinated. "So then you made a bathful — "

"No, we didn't. Louise just smashed the basin to smithereens. It was just after she'd been psychoanalyzed, and she was scared stiff of repressing herself. Not that she ever *had,* so far as I could see; but she said yes, and if she'd only known sooner there wouldn't be a whole plate left in the Café Royal." Julia paused and looked at Sir William anxiously. "She isn't *rough,* you know; it's just that she's got a rather quick temper."

"She sounds a most delightful and entertaining companion," said Sir William. "I won't say I'm sorry she can't come with us to-night, because I want you to myself; but when we're in London I shall have great pleasure in meeting her."

Julia looked at him adoringly.

"You don't know how lovely that is, William. I'd hate to drop her, and I'd hate to have to see her behind your back — in fact I wouldn't, because I've promised myself I'll never know anyone you don't like. You'll never have to be ashamed of my friends, William — truly you won't!"

"I'm sure I shan't," said Sir William.

He spoke sincerely; he had long made up his mind to the fact that marriage with Julia would undoubtedly bring him some very queer acquaintances; but he was also convinced that her instinct for people could be perfectly trusted. Her friends might be what she called "rum"; they would also be what she called "good sorts." Their company would probably be extremely entertaining, and he had no fear of their influence, for Julia was too clever to let him be either bored or swindled. His only apprehension was that she might plunge to the other extreme and demand to open bazaars. Well, if she wanted to, she could. Sir William felt that even Julia's respectability would have something lavish and cheerful about it — like a Costers' open-air service. . . .

"You'd make a first-rate Pearlie Queen," he told her; and suddenly wondered how many of his own acquaintances, given that remark, would be able to guess the context — *Sir William to the future Lady Waring.*

"Not a single one of them!" cried Julia, when he had explained why he was laughing. She thought the matter over and became slightly indignant. "And they won't even when they've seen me, either. I'm going to be the perfect lady."

Sir William bent and kissed her.

"Whether I like it or not?"

"Whether you like it or not," said Julia firmly.

Five minutes later she was being kissed again, this time by Fred Genocchio.

### 3

It happened in this way: Julia, anxious to see whether her taffeta needed ironing, went down to the house alone and was met on the upper terrace by Anthelmine and the woman from the lodge. They were evidently looking for her; they had a visiting-card, which Anthelmine seized out of her companion's hand and thrust with a flourish under Julia's eye.

It was Fred Genocchio's.

For a moment Julia stood still, a prey to the most violent and conflicting emotions. Astonishment came first, then dismay, then a wave of flattered excitement. She didn't want Fred any more, especially she didn't want him there and then; but how touching of him to have come! Poor old Fred!

"Where is he?" she asked. *"Où est-il?"*

"*Là-bas*," replied Anthelmine, jerking her shoulder towards the gates. She looked at Julia with a friendly, conspiratorial smile; she was evidently aware that the visitor had nothing to do with Sir William.

"*Je vais*," said Julia haughtily. "*Merci beaucoup.*" Anthelmine smiled again, and with a lavish display of tact hustled her companion in the direction of the kitchen door. Julia waited till they were gone, then hurried down the drive. *Dear* old Fred! she thought, as she rounded the bend; she would speak to him for just five minutes, very kindly and superiorly, before sending him away. She could do no less. Not to do as much would be rude, unladylike. In her anxiety to get it over Julia almost ran, so that Mr. Genocchio, watching from below, and with no clue to her real motive, may be excused for misinterpreting the situation. He saw Julia hastening towards him, catching her skirt on a rose trail, jerking it free and hastening on; and with happy (though unjustified) confidence stepped forward and caught her in his arms and kissed her soundly.

"Fred!" cried Julia.

He at once released her. There was no mistaking that repulsive note. Julia backed a little away and held out her hand.

"Why, Fred!" she said graciously. "This *is* a surprise!"

But his mental agility was not equal to hers. Instead
of shaking hands like a gentleman, Mr. Genocchio
merely gaped.

"What's up?" he asked bluntly. "Aren't you pleased
to see me?"

"Of course I'm pleased to see you."

"Well, you don't seem like it."

"I'm surprised," explained Julia. "I thought you were
in Paris. Is the trip over?"

"Yes, it's over," said Mr. Genocchio glumly. "Ma and
the others went back yesterday."

"Is Ma all right now?"

"Yes, she's all right."

"And the others?"

"They're all right too. What about yourself?"

"Oh, I'm all right," said Julia.

"You look it," said Mr. Genocchio. "You look grand."
The old admiration was warm in his voice, bright
in his eyes, and in spite of herself Julia could not
repress a slight responsive glow. He *was* beautifully
built, even in an ordinary suit. If he had turned up in
tights she could hardly have answered for herself. . . .

"Having a good time here?"

"Lovely," said Julia.

"You don't want a change? I mean, you wouldn't
like to run over to Aix or somewhere — or even back
to Paris — for a day or two?"

Julia took a long breath.

"I ought to tell you, Fred, — I ought to have told you at once, — I'm going to be married."

Mr. Genocchio stared at her a moment in silence, then turned on his heel and stared at a rosebush instead.

"Congratulations," he said over his shoulder. "Chap staying here, I suppose?"

"Yes. Don't look like that, Fred!"

"Why not?"

"It — it upsets me."

"I'm upset myself," said Mr. Genocchio. "I know I've no right to be, but there it is." He broke off a rose switch and stood turning it in his hands. "I'd hired a car," he said.

Julia sniffed. She had so indefensibly sympathetic a nature that in another moment she would have wept.

"I'm ever so sorry, Fred. I am truly."

"Nothing to be sorry about," said Mr. Genocchio, recovering himself. "At least, I don't suppose there is. Is he a good sort?"

The phrase, so totally inadequate to Sir William, jarred on Julia's ear. But an odd shyness, a sort of modesty, prevented her from explaining the true magnificence of her prospects. As she would have put it herself, she didn't want to rub it in. . . .

"One of the best, Fred. I've been damned lucky."

"I know who's got the luck all right," muttered

Mr. Genocchio. "Well, it's all in the game. I suppose I'd better be going."

Julia hesitated. It seemed awful to let him come all that way and not offer him so much as a drink; but what was the good? He wouldn't be comfortable, nor would she. Indeed, when she thought of introducing him to the Packetts, and particularly to Susan, discomfort was altogether too mild a word. It would be plain bloody awful, and no offence to anyone. . . .

"I see I had," said Mr. Genocchio slowly. "I've put you out by coming. I'm sorry."

If only he could have swung off, glorious on his trapeze, and disappeared to the ruffle of drums! If only he could have leapt into his car and rushed away at sixty miles an hour! But twenty feet of gravel path separated him even from the gate, and that was too high to be vaulted. It was the worst exit he had ever been faced with: all he could do was to get himself off . . .

In Julia too the sense of anticlimax was strong. It was so strong as to be unbearable. All her theatrical instincts, as well as her genuine fondness for the man, rose in revolt. She caught him by the shoulder, turned him round, and held up her face to be kissed.

"Julie!"

"Fred, darling!"

He held her tight ("I hope that's not another bruise,"

thought Julia, already assuaged), then almost pushed her from him and hurried off. Julia too turned away, and without looking back again to reascend the drive. As far as the first landing complacency accompanied her: she felt she had handled the situation well, artistically — which meant that she had got the last ounce out of it — and, above all, in a ladylike manner. She was very much pleased with herself. But as she arrived in sight of the house, this agreeable mood changed. She felt a curious sensation of having burned her boats. That was odd and unpleasant enough, but the feeling that succeeded it was worse still. An awful doubt invaded Julia's mind. Would a lady — a real lady — have offered that last kiss without being asked? Above all, would she have *enjoyed* it? Considering these two questions carefully, Julia was forced to answer yes to the first (because Fred wanted it so badly, and it would have been a shame to refuse) and no to the second. This was very bad, since she herself had enjoyed it thoroughly. She had enjoyed it just as much as if she hadn't been engaged to Sir William at all.

"I'm awful," thought Julia, with sincere melancholy.

But she repented. She repented hard, all evening, until it was time to start for Aix; and then the sight of Sir William in tails drove everything else from her head.

# Chapter 23

After an evening of unalloyed pleasure Julia and Sir William returned to the villa at one in the morning. They had dined, they had danced a little, but chiefly they had watched the people — Julia as usual keeping up a running commentary on everyone and everything she saw, Sir William as usual listening and laughing at her flights. To Julia's delight, they saw the Disgusted Lady, who, marvellous in ice-blue slipper-satin, engrossed and despised the services of the best professional partner while her companion of the Pernollet admired from the edge of the floor. "Isn't she grand?" demanded Julia. "Astounding," agreed Sir William; "a collector's piece." And Julia beamed at him, because that was just what she had tried to convey to Susan, and he understood so exactly. She was looking well herself, too; she drew many admiring glances; while as for Sir William — "You're the most distinguished man here!" declared Julia. "Look as fond of me as you can, William!" And Sir William did look fond of her, just as though he were a Frenchman — except that everyone was taking him (Julia knew it) for an English lord. . . .

At Muzin Sir William put the car away in its barn, so as not to wake the house, and they walked up together through the still garden. A full moon dropped silver between the trees, robbing with its brightness all brightness of colour, paling the red roses, darkening the white, but exquisitely defining, by a stroke of silverpoint and a line of charcoal, every bough and twig that daylight merged in green. Julia stood still and let the scarf slip from her shoulders. At once the moonlight flowed over them, making them whiter than milk.

"What a wonderful night!"

"Wonderful," echoed Sir William. "Whenever there's a full moon, my dear, you must wear that frock."

Julia spread out her wide skirt and let the light play over it. It was no longer blue, but black and silver.

"I'll always have one like it," she promised. "I — I'll be buried in it, William." Suddenly her voice and her hands trembled, the stiff folds dropped together with a long rustling sigh. "William!" she said. "William — I'm frightened!"

At once, as when she came running panic-stricken from the woods, the barrier of his arm held her safe.

"Frightened? Why frightened now, my darling?"

"Because it's too good. It can't last."

"Nonsense," said Sir William gently. "It's going to last all our lives."

"Then you'll die first, and I shan't be able to bear it. Or something will happen to stop us."

"Nonsense," said Sir William again. "You're tired, my dear, and excited. All this business has been a strain on you, and to-morrow I'm going to put an end to it. We'll be married straight away."

But Julia did not hear. She had started, turned away from him, and was staring into the shadows by the house.

"Something moved!" she whispered. "There's someone there!"

Sir William took three long steps from her side and laid his hand against the dark wall.

"No one," he said. "Come in, my dear; you're imagining things."

He led her into the house and turned on the hall lights. Safe within four walls, Julia was able to look up at him and laugh while he chided her for her foolishness. Then she kissed him good night and went into her room and sat down before the mirror. Her reflection glowed back at her, flushed of cheek and bright of eye; her shoulders —

Her shoulders!

"There!" said Julia aloud. "If I haven't left my scarf outside!"

## 2

It was a nice scarf — it had been really good — and the dew would ruin it. Julia jumped up and went to the door, meaning to ask Sir William to fetch it in for her; but once in the lobby she paused. She had a feeling that Sir William might not like to be caught in his pants; she fancied him rather particular about that sort of thing. In the end she went out herself, and indeed had not far to go, for the scarf lay just at the foot of the porch steps. Julia picked it up, turned to reascend, and all at once felt her heart stand still.

Something *had* moved. Something was moving then.

A shadow detached itself from the shadows, took on an outline, showed a face white in the moonlight. It found a bitter and sardonic voice.

"So I wish you joy?" said Bryan Relton.

Instinctively, as though warding off a blow, Julia put out her hand. "Wait!" the gesture said. "Don't hurt me just yet! Wait!"

But he would not wait. His voice went on, hard and mocking.

"So you're going to marry him, Julia? You're going to purge and live cleanly and be Lady Waring? Do you remember what you said yesterday, Julia? Do you remember what you said to me in the vine, and what you've been saying to me for weeks — Julia darling?"

His questions pelted her like stones. She retreated before them till she stood with her back to the wall.

"Stop!" she whispered harshly. "Be quiet! You don't understand —"

Bryan looked at her and laughed.

"I understand very well indeed: when it came to the point he was too big a fish to let go. But don't think I blame you, my dear, for aren't we the same sort? Don't we both take what we can get?"

Julia moistened her lips.

"Not Susan," she said. "Not Susan!"

"Not if I can get her, darling? Isn't she still engaged to me? She wouldn't have been to-morrow, of course — I've been running wild all day — thinking how noble you were, Julia! — rehearsing my part for the renunciation scene. I've been running wild in the moonlight — and how fortunately it's turned out! You've opened my eyes, Julia; I can see now what a fool you nearly made of me. Why shouldn't I have Susan, if I can get her?"

"Because it won't last," said Julia more steadily. "It wouldn't last two years. . . ."

"Then I shall have had them. As you say, my dear, two years will probably be enough for both of us. I believe you'll miss me more than anyone, Julia; you'll never find a son-in-law so much your own sort again."

At last Julia moved. She dragged herself away from the wall and set her foot on the porch step. She had to pass close to Bryan to do so, but she did not look at him.

"You're not my sort at all," she said. "You're bad."

Then she fled into the house, into her own room, and sat down once more before the table with the mirror.

### 3

Her reflection looked quite different. In ten minutes it seemed to have grown old. But Julia did not study it long, for she had a great deal to do.

In the first place, she had to pack.

It was strange — this struck her afterwards, when she was back in London — how little difficulty she had in making up her mind. Or rather, she did not make it up at all: she simply saw before her a series of pre-ordained actions, like a part in a play, which had inevitably to be performed. The reasons for them she left aside: even the thought of Susan was colourless and remote.

She had to pack, get out of the house unobserved, and pick up a lift on the Paris road. At that time of year there were always cars making an early start from Aix; one of them — preferably a fast tourer driven by a solitary man — would stop for her at the Muzin fork. It would be just another of her gay adventures. . . .

"I ought to get some sleep," thought Julia.

But she could not. The short night passed without her closing her eyes. First, slowly and clumsily, she filled both her suitcases; then, realizing that they would be too heavy to carry, decided to take only one. That meant unpacking both and starting again. She was very slow about it; every now and then she found herself standing motionless, with a stocking in her hand, or a nightgown over her arm; and how long she had been thus transfixed, or why, she did not know. About four o'clock her knees gave under her; she lay down on the smooth bed and turned off the light. But the room was not dark, it was grey with the twilight of early morning, and in a panic lest day should surprise her Julia pulled herself once more to her feet. Fortunately there was something she could do. She was still wearing her taffeta dress; she had forgotten to pack it, and now left it just where it fell, a heap of blackness on the white floor. She bathed her face and arms in cold water, put on her linen suit, and sat half an hour trying to make rouge and lipstick look natural instead of ghastly. Then she was ready. She decided not to take her big coat, as it was rather shabby. She thought she would look gayer without it.

There remained one other thing to be done, and it was the hardest.

My dearest William [wrote Julia], I am very sorry, but I'm not going to marry you, so this is to say good-bye.

The words looked silly to her, but she could think of no others. She stared at them till they had lost all meaning, then folded the paper in two and went out to slip it under Sir William's door.

The lobby, because of its shuttered window, was still dark; Julia suddenly remembered the night of the thunderstorm. She had stood in just the same place, outside Sir William's room, trembling as she trembled now. "What was I so unhappy about?" Julia wondered. "I couldn't have known *then?*" She put the puzzle from her mind and performed the next in the series of necessary actions. She walked to the front door, slid back the bolt, and let herself out. The action after that was to take the lower path, beside the kitchen-garden, thus avoiding the village, and pass through its wicket. Mechanically Julia did so. There was no one stirring. She walked the quarter of a mile to where the road from Muzin forked into the highway. Aix lay to her left, Paris somewhere to her right. Julia dropped her suitcase in the dust, and sat down on it to wait.

# Chapter 24

The Misses Marlowe prided themselves on being expert travellers in general, and particularly, when motoring, on their habit of making early starts. "From six till nine," Miss Marlowe often explained to an interested circle at Wimbledon, "one gets *cool* air and a *clear* road" — in addition to which both she and her sister definitely enjoyed the sensation of leaving their hotel while everyone else was asleep. They felt they had stolen a march on time, and especially on their fellow guests. The French, indeed, often made early starts too; but the Misses Marlowe regularly led both English and Americans.

It thus happened that at ten minutes to seven Julia, still watching by the Muzin fork, had to change her position and get behind the hedge. The old Daimler was easily recognizable: she had no wish that its occupants should recognize her. They would certainly give her a lift, but they would also want to know too much about her three children. Nevertheless Julia

— 299 —

looked after them longingly; her spirits were low, her body was stiff, and so far she had had no luck. Of the three cars that had passed already, one had contained a mutually absorbed couple, one a large family party (with perambulator strapped on top), and the third had been going so fast that it nearly ran over her.

"I ought to start and walk to Belley," thought Julia; and with the resolution of despair — like a shipwrecked mariner stepping off a raft and beginning to swim — took a few quick steps along the dusty road. But her knees felt curiously weak; she stopped, turned, and took a last look behind. Another car had just rounded the curve and was approaching at no great speed: a disreputable, two-seater Citroën, it was not at all the sort of vehicle she had hoped for; but at least it was driven by a single male. Julia stepped out into the middle of the road and waved an arm; as the car slowed down she saw that this driver was a very young man indeed — younger even than Bryan; his hair, his complexion, and his burberry proclaimed him an Anglo-Saxon. "That's something," Julia encouraged herself. "Anyway he'll understand what I say. He'll love me. He'll think I'm an adventuress."

The Citroën came to a stop. She advanced towards it and put a foot on the running-board.

She said, "Can you give me a lift?"

The young man looked at her. It was a queer look —

not fresh, more puzzled; and there was something in it which Julia could not recognize.

"Where do you want to go?" he asked.

"I don't care," said Julia baldly. That wasn't what she had meant to say. She had meant to say "Follow the sun!" or "Your way is mine!"—something gay and adventurous like that; but the three miserable words slipped out before she knew. With a great effort she gave him one of her good-old-Julia smiles, and asked where he was bound for.

"Well, Paris, eventually," said the young man; "but I don't quite know when I shall get there. This car isn't particularly reliable."

"It's reliable enough for me," said Julia, heaving her suitcase on to the edge of the dickey. The young man hesitated a moment, then with another odd glance climbed out, placed the suitcase more securely, and opened the car door. Remarking on the heat, he also took off his burberry; and this surprised Julia, who was shivering, until he clumsily wrapped it round her knees. With a sigh of relief she sank back against the cushions: she had pulled it off, she had done it again; and automatically she felt for her powder-box. But she made no use of it. There was a mirror in the lid, and the sight of her reflected face told her suddenly, brutally, the meaning of the young man's glance.

He was giving her a lift not because he thought she

was an adventuress, but because she looked such a tired, tear-stained, unhappy old woman.

## 2

It was just after eight o'clock when Sir William in the Daimler turned down the fork from Muzin onto the main road. Julia had thus scarcely more than seventy minutes' start of him, and the difference in speed between the two cars was considerable. The Citroën averaged twenty-two miles an hour, the Daimler forty-three. Unluckily, from Sir William's point of view, they were travelling in opposite directions.

Sir William drove towards Aix. He was not at this time unduly anxious; Julia's note had upset him, because he knew how distressed she must have been when she wrote it; but it had by no means produced despair. He drove at moderate speed, half-expecting to overtake her, either afoot or in a car, on the actual road; knowing Julia to be penniless, and to a certain extent following her thoughts, he had never had a moment's doubt of her destination. She would try to get to Paris, and thence back to London: therefore she required either money for a railway ticket, or a lift in a car; and Aix (Sir William now knew all about Mr. Rickaby) was her obvious hunting-ground. His mistake, of course, lay in underestimating the simplicity of Julia's plan: it had not occurred to him that she would merely stand by the roadside and try to get to Paris direct. Even with his knowledge of her, he believed she would need at least half a day to establish, so to speak, her connections, and his chief speculation was as to the sort of company in which he would find her doing it.

Having failed to overtake Julia on the road, Sir William breakfasted in Aix, outside a *pâtisserie,* where he could watch the passers-by, and spent the next hour in a methodical survey of the chief cafés and streets. It was therefore not until half-past ten that the Daimler, at full speed, once more passed the Muzin fork and took the Paris road.

### 3

About thirty miles out of Bourg the Misses Marlowe, being driven at their usual placid rate of twenty-seven miles an hour, overtook a small and very noisy Citroën. The time was half-past ten, for they had stopped in the town to sustain themselves with a good breakfast.

"I shouldn't like to drive in that," observed Miss Marlowe. "It sounds as though it's going to break down."

With unusual agility her sister twisted round on the seat to stare out of the back window.

"But did you see who was in it?" she cried. "That nice woman we took into Aix!"

"Well!" said Miss Marlowe, also pulling herself up for a look. "That's surely not her husband driving!"

"No, he's quite young. Besides, we saw *them* go off in a Daimler — from the Pernollet. How very odd!"

The incident afforded them an interesting topic of conversation all the way to Saulieu, where they lunched rather too well at the Hôtel de Poste.

## 4

Lunch at the villa was served to Susan and her grandmother alone. They were both rather silent; the curious tale brought by Claudia occupied their thoughts but tied their tongues. The young Madame Packett, said Claudia, must have left very early indeed, she was not in her room at half-past seven, and her bed had not been slept in; the Monsieur did not leave till eight o'clock. She, Claudia, had had to wake him up to give him his early tea, and the note she found on the floor. . . .

"And he left no message?" asked Mrs. Packett.

None at all, said Claudia. He went like a gust of wind. He enquired was the big car still in the barn, and she ran down and looked, and ran back to say it was, and there! — he was ready to depart!

"It sounds like a paper-chase," said Susan, with a rare attempt at lightness. Something had happened which she did not understand, and instinctively she was trying to minimize it. But in truth she was deeply disturbed; there had been another incident, — of which her grandmother knew nothing, — the implications of which she herself was not yet ready to face. Bryan had been with them in the hall while Claudia started her tale; without a word he had gone straight to Julia's room, flung open the door, slammed it to again, and walked out of the house. Susan had waited till Mrs. Packett was gone, and then repeated his actions; she saw nothing but a blue taffeta dress lying in a heap on the floor. The sight did not strike her as odd, — Julia was always untidy, — and for a moment she stood puzzled: the look on Bryan's face had prepared her almost for Julia's corpse. Then, without quite knowing why, she ran out through the house, and down the drive, and seeing Bryan at the gate called to ask where he was going.

"To look for Julia," said Bryan shortly.

"But — but it's absurd!" cried Susan. She was quite close to him now, there was only the gate between them. The sound of her raised voice startled her; she lowered it, and tried to speak reasonably. "It's absurd, Bryan! Julia isn't a lost child!"

His answer was completely irrelevant. As he turned

and hurried on, over his shoulder, he said brusquely: —

"By the way — I've had a cable. I've got to go home to-night."

That was all. Susan went back to the house and occupied her morning, as usual, with the plays of Racine. She was not quite certain that she had heard aright. In any case, when Mrs. Packett, at luncheon, enquired why Bryan was not there, she said merely that he had gone off for one of his long walks.

But she knew, all the same, that something had happened to her.

## 5

Julia and the young man lunched at a small café at Arney-le-Duc, and the young man paid. Julia let him. There was nothing else she could do. She hadn't spirit enough even to tell him a tale or two in exchange. She had so far made not the slightest attempt to account for herself, nor did she do so during the long, hot, dusty afternoon. She simply sat, tongue-tied and wretched, not even hearing when her companion produced one of his brief, uncomfortable remarks. She sat like a woman in a trance, or a woman half-dead; her face was so queerly blank that the young man, in his alarm, turned off from the Paris road at Auxerre and drove into the town to procure her a cup of tea. He had great faith in tea where women were concerned

— his own mother, the widowed head of a large family, was regularly revived by it five times a day. The idea was a sound one, but from his own point of view unfortunate, since Sir William's Daimler was now only twenty miles behind. Had the Citroën kept to the main road, it would have been overtaken in less than an hour, and the young man's responsibility would at once have come to a welcome end. But he turned aside; Sir William drove on; and the chance was lost.

Outside the Café de la République Julia drank her tea in silence. It did her a certain amount of good; it made her a little more able to comprehend, if not to take an interest in, her immediate surroundings. These were highly picturesque; they had been admired (the young man told her) by Walter Pater. Something in his voice made Julia look, not at the roof-line, but at him; and for the first time she realized that he was extremely worried.

"Look here," he stammered, at once abandoning the scenery to profit by what no doubt appeared to him a glimmering of intelligence, "Look here — I'm most frightfully sorry — "

"I know," said Julia wearily. "I'm a damned nuisance to you."

The young man turned crimson.

"You're not in the least. I hate driving alone. Only — the fact of the matter is — I've been running it rather fine. I mean, I've got exactly enough cash to get me to Paris — for food and petrol and so on. I mean, it's just enough for one. You see — "

"That's all right," said Julia. "I understand. You've been sweet to bring me as far as this. As a matter of fact — " she racked her tired brain for some convincing story — "I've got friends here. Staying here. I'll be quite all right now."

It didn't convince the young man. He stared in front of him, his forehead still wrinkled, and said uncomfortably: —

"Look here — this may be cheek on my part — but why don't you go to a consul? There isn't one nearer than Paris, but if we went to an hotel we could make them ring him up."

Julia reached across the table, took a cigarette out of the young man's packet, and let him light it for her. To go to a consul, in her mind, was like going to the workhouse — it meant you were so down and out there was nothing left for you but public assistance. "All right," thought Julia, "I'll take it. I've got to. I've got to get back somehow. . . ."

"They're doing it every day," said the young man, with a kind of clumsy tact. "I mean, sending people home. A friend of mine got stuck last year, at Genoa. Another chap I know was stuck at Paris. It's ten to one I shall be stuck there myself."

"All right," repeated Julia aloud. "You move off, and I'll go along straightaway."

"I'll come with you."

"No," said Julia, at last managing a smile. "I'll look more distressed by myself. Distressed British Subject — that's my line now."

The young man stood up, felt in his pocket, and produced a handful of crumpled ten-franc notes.

"If you try leaving any of those with me," said Julia, "I — I'll get back into the car!"

To make his farewells easier, she pretended to be very busy doing her face. It took her a long time; and when she looked up again, she was quite alone.

## 6

Like the young man's mother, like every other Eng lishwoman at half-past four in the afternoon, the Misses Marlowe wanted their tea.

"If I don't get a cup soon, I shall go to sleep," complained the elder. "It's this dreadful heat."

"It's the lunch," said her sister more realistically. "But we'll be at Joigny in ten minutes, and there's a place there."

"A *nice* place?" asked Miss Marlowe wistfully.

"A.A.," replied Miss Ann.

The two ladies sat forward in their seats, eagerly

scanning the railway line for the first sign of the bridge.

On crossing it, as Sir William did half an hour later, all drivers must slow down; the Modern Hotel stands directly and invitingly in front of them. Sir William looked at it and realized that his throat was exceedingly dry. He had been driving now, with a brief interval for lunch, for something like eight hours, and anxiety had taken possession of him. Among his fears was the dread that he might have developed a blind spot — that his eye, automatically observing every car on the road, might have ceased to transmit its messages to the brain. There was another car to be observed now, a very old Daimler standing outside the hotel; Sir William looked at it with extreme care, and this time at least his eye made no mistake.

It was the car Julia had shown him, outside the Pernollet, as belonging to two old ladies who had once given her a lift.

Sir William drew up beside it, climbed stiffly out, and entered the hotel just as the Misses Marlowe were paying for their tea. Julia was not with them. He stood a moment on the threshold, trying to frame some question which he could reasonably ask of them, resentfully aware — for he had lost all sense of humour — that owing to Julia's reprehensible habits he did not even know what name they knew her by. Then, while he hesitated, the two ladies looked up and caught sight of him.

"*Oh!*" cried the Misses Marlowe in unison. "We've seen your wife!"

Without waiting to be invited Sir William walked over and sat down at their table. For some reason it was evidently expected that he should be anxious: the two ladies showed no surprise at his lack of ceremony.

"Young men are so reckless!" exclaimed the elder. "Hasn't she got back yet?"

"No," said Sir William, his mind all at once alert and busy. A young man — there was nothing surprising about that! But where did the recklessness come in? "Were they breaking the speed limit?" he asked. "I know on these roads — "

"No, indeed!" exclaimed Miss Marlowe. "They could hardly get along. And the car made such peculiar noises — "

"*Spluttering* noises — " put in her sister.

" — that we were really quite alarmed."

"So am I," admitted Sir William. "In fact, I'm looking for them now. This young man — a young acquaintance of ours — insisted on taking my wife for a run, and I'm afraid they may have had a breakdown. Could you tell me exactly where you saw them?"

"Not far out of Bourg," said Miss Marlowe promptly, "but that was about half-past ten. If they kept to the

Paris road they ought to be somewhere behind us. Where were they going?"

"Oh, some beauty-spot or other," said Sir William vaguely. If they really were on that road, why hadn't he passed them? The blind spot, after all? Had Julia seen him go by — and made no sign?

"Auxerre?" suggested Miss Ann. "If your wife is fond of Pater — "

In spite of fatigue and anxiety, Sir William smiled: he made a mental note that he must one day give Julia *Marius,* and see what happened. . . .

"That's very likely," he said aloud. "I ought to have thought of it myself: it's the only place where I could have missed them. I think" — he pulled himself up again — "I'll go back there now."


### 7

Driving slowly through the picturesque streets of Auxerre, Sir William saw a small disreputable car move splutteringly off from before a small deserted café. It had only one occupant, but he was a young man such as the Misses Marlowe had described. Sir William accelerated, found himself jammed by a slow-moving cart, and changing his mind came to a sudden stop. He could catch the Citroën easily; in the meantime he got out and crossed over to the Café de la République. On the other side of the privet hedge, at an empty table, sat a woman with her elbows among the crockery and her head on her fists.

"Julia!" said Sir William.

Julia looked up, her mouth and eyes opened, she made a queer, flurried movement as though she were trying to conceal herself behind her hands. Sir William walked up to her and leant heavily on the table.

"My dear Julia!" he said. "What on earth will you do next?"

THE END